SHOOT-OUT

"Drop your rifle, Mr. Snell!" Maude said hoarsely. "At once." She was behind the counter, with a shotgun leveled at Snell's belly. "I can put a ten-inch hole in you at this range, Mr. Snell!"

With his left hand he dropped the Sharps rifle back against the wall; with his right he reached for his revolver. In the instant of will that brought her to press the trigger, Maude saw Julie crouching close to the wall behind the big man, and in that instant she shifted her aim. He was hit with scatter shot in the leg above the knee, cursing as blood stained into the greasy cloth above his boot top.

Shaken by the gun's recoil, Maude remembered too late to reload. Snell drew his revolver, took deliberate aim, and fired. The bullet struck her in the chest. She coughed softly, then her legs crumbled as she slid out of sight.

The Girl from
Fort Wicked

The Girl from Fort Wicked

DEE BROWN

A DELL BOOK

Published by
Dell Publishing
a division of
The Bantam Doubleday Dell Publishing Group, Inc.
666 Fifth Avenue
New York, New York 10103

ISBN: 0-440-20218-3

Printed in the United States of America

Published simultaneously in Canada

November 1988

10 9 8 7 6 5 4 3 2 1

KRI

For
J. M. B.

The Girl from Fort Wicked

1

Headquarters Yellowhorse Command
Sun River Cantonment, June 19.

ASSISTANT ADJUTANT GENERAL
Department of the Platte.

SIR: I have respectfully to report that a wagon train proceeding from Newcomb's Wells to this headquarters was attacked by hostile Indians on the 18th instant near Clear Creek ravine. Detachments of two companies, B and H, 12th Cavalry, acting as escort were forced to engage the enemy on ground where it would have been impossible to have maneuvered cavalry. Captain Carter in command and Lieutenant Dickey were both seriously wounded and put out of action in the first engagement. Two noncommisioned officers made the best resistance they could, but Major Daly the paymaster and two civilian drivers, and a female passenger identified as Miss Anna Llewellyn of Massachusetts were killed. The paymaster was carrying upward of $6000 for payment of troops this command. An undetermined number of new rifles and carbines in shipment were also taken by the raiders. Troop C, 12th Cavalry, under command Captain Benjamin Westcott is now in the field in pursuit of the hostiles. Captain Westcott is . . .

* * *

First Sergeant Michael Connors pulled his mount in closer to the scout, Peter Dunreath, and said: "The capt'n's takin' it too hard."

Dunreath grunted, but the only movement of his muscles was the blinking of half-closed eyes against sun glare as he kept his gaze fixed down the line of Arapaho tepees to where Captain Westcott was standing.

Five squaws were lined up in front of Westcott. A pair of dismounted troopers, carbines at ready, stood on either side of them.

The squaws were wearing fancy Eastern dresses—silks and frilled satins and one that was obviously a bridal gown. A few hours ago the dresses had been packed in a trunk belonging to Anna Llewellyn of Massachusetts.

Under the hot noonday sun, Westcott stood tall and rigid as a parade-ground soldier, staring down at the squaws. His battered campaign hat swung from one hand. His shock of hair was red as fire in the cruel sunlight. His eyes held no expression; their normal bright blue looked dead and burned out.

To Westcott's left, along a narrow strip of grassy creek bank, were the other Arapahoes—women, children, and old men—held in close check by a detail of troopers.

From out of this restless mass a papoose squawled suddenly, breaking the stillness, and then Westcott turned toward his mount, reaching for his saber. The metal flashed in the sun.

"Watch out," Sergeant Connors whispered quickly to Dunreath.

Dunreath brushed his fingers across the stubby beard around his tobacco-stained lips. "I better get down there," he said mildly, "or Ben Westcott will hate hisself in the mornin'."

"The capt'n was never one for squaw killin'," Connors went on worriedly. "Still if she'd been my girl, that Miss Llewellyn—"

"He's never said a word," Dunreath added, and nudged his gray mount gently into motion. As he rode along the line of tepees, he watched Westcott turn back to the squaws, the saber glinting like silver.

One of the squaws began wailing. She was wearing a gay blue frock with lace along the sleeves. She kneeled on the ground, facing Westcott. The captain leaned forward slightly, holding the saber extended until she rose again, and then he eased the tip into the thin blue cloth, ripping it away from her shoulders.

Dunreath halted his horse a dozen yards behind the captain, watching without comment. He glanced back quickly to where

Connors waited in front of the line of dismounted troopers on the slope.

Westcott continued his slashing at the blue dress until the squaw flinched and dropped down on her knees again. The captain swore then, dropped the saber, and stepped in close to the woman. He made a motion with his bare hand, then checked himself, as if he could not bear to touch the ripped cloth. He stood erect again and took his gauntlets from inside his shirt and put them on.

With his gauntleted hands Westcott began ripping the dress from the squaw, each motion more savage than the other, dropping the torn pieces of cloth on the ground until the woman stood bare-breasted with only a red calico underskirt over her lower body. He turned to the others then, mechanically stripping the stolen dresses from them until all were left only their red and orange petticoats and underskirts.

Dunreath shook his head slowly, and shifted in his saddle. Again, as he had been doing all morning, he scanned the horizon, wondering where the warriors were, how many there were, and how fresh their horses. He heard Westcott's voice, like a rasp: "Throw that on the fire!"

The captain had moved over to a boiling cooking pot in front of one of the tepees. He booted the black pot over on its side, and prodded the fire into a blaze. "Connors!"

"Yes, sir!" Sergeant Connors' voice boomed loud down the slope.

"Bring down a searching party. They may have rifles hidden in the lodges."

The two troopers were gathering up the shredded dresses, dropping the rags on the fire which smoldered for a minute, the smoke stinking of scorching cloth, and then blazed brightly. Westcott turned his back on it.

He looks all right now, Dunreath thought, *except for his eyes and that gray line along his mouth.*

Westcott noticed Dunreath for the first time. "I told you to stay back up there," Westcott said.

"I can't see so good any more," Dunreath replied, and then grinned. "Unless I'm up close."

Westcott didn't smile. "Get over to that mob and see what

you can find out from the old men. We can't stay here all day.
We've got to find the warriors."

Not with our horses worn down like they are, Dunreath
thought. *He's still half crazy. Maybe I would be, too, if that'd
been my girl.* The scout dismounted and led his horse between
two tepees toward a sapling.

Before he finished looping his tie rope, Dunreath noticed the
scalp. It was stretched on a hoop suspended from a pole at the
rear of the larger tepee, drying in hot sunlight. The light gave
the hair a gold sheen. From the ringlets and the length he knew
it was a white woman's scalp.

Without breaking his motion, Dunreath loosened a rope behind his saddle, slid his blanket out, and walked toward the
drying scalp. He had dropped the blanket over the hoop when
he heard Westcott behind him. The captain's breath caught in
his throat, whatever words he was about to say strangled in a
hoarse exhalation.

Westcott brushed the scout aside, and jerked the blanket
away from the hoop. Flies buzzed in an angry cloud.

The captain stood with his legs wide apart, his erect shoulders drooping a little, staring at the scalp with the same expres-
sionless glare he had fixed upon the squaws a few moments ago.

Dunreath touched Westcott's shoulder. "Don't pry into it,
Ben," he said gently, and asked: "What do you want done with
it?"

"Burn it." Westcott's voice was like a file against hard metal.
He turned his back on the thing, blinked at the buffalo symbols
on the tepee, and started striding toward the group of
Arapahoes along the creek bank. Dunreath lifted the drying
hoop, and as he followed Westcott he dropped it on the blazing
heap of shredded dresses. The five half-naked squaws still cow-
ered in the shade of the tepees.

Several papooses were squawling now in the close-packed
crowd. The willows offered little shade, and the midday heat
made the Indians restless. The troopers also were uneasy, prod-
ding with their carbines at any moving body around the edges
of the group.

Westcott had halted, and was motioning the troopers to bring
out one of the old men. An Indian, naked but for a pair of
blanket-cloth trousers, lurched forward hesitantly. His dirty

hair was cropped at the shoulders. His arms were bony, the flesh corded with knotted veins.

"Ask him the name of the warrior," Westcott ordered sharply, "who lives in the large tepee with buffalo markings."

"We better sit him down in the shade first," Dunreath replied easily, and motioned toward a broken log downstream. Westcott frowned with impatience, and then followed Dunreath and the old Arapaho to the shaded log. The scout held his closed hand out, moving it downward, and the old man sat.

With signs and a word or two of Arapaho, Dunreath asked the question. The old man shook his head. Dunreath squatted in front of him, patiently repeating his interrogation. With a gesture of indifference, the Indian replied in Arapaho. Dunreath repeated the words, and added in English: "Black Horn?"

The old man nodded slowly, and said something else in Arapaho.

"It's Black Horn's tepee," Dunreath said to Westcott. "Sub-chief of the Greasy Faces band. The old man says one of them squaws you insulted by disrobin' her in public is Black Horn's woman."

"Which woman is Black Horn's?" As he spoke, Westcott glanced back at the half-naked squaws. He rubbed one hand hard over his rumpled red hair, and his lips tightened over his teeth.

"What difference it make, Ben?" Dunreath replied quietly. "That wouldn't fix nothin'."

"Right now I wish to God I was an Indian. Breach for a breach, eye for an eye." Westcott's jaw squeezed shut as he turned his back on the squaws.

Behind them came the clatter of First Sergeant Connors' detail, beginning their search through the lodges. Tin pans rattled and troopers shouted as they turned up rifles hidden under blankets, and brought them out to stack in neat military fashion in the center of the village. The rifles were ancient, most of them rusted. The warriors had taken the new ones captured from the train, leaving their old ones behind with the squaws.

"Ask him where his chief, Wolf Moccasin, is now," Westcott said.

Wolf Moccasin, the old man said, was hunting deer with the

Sagebrush warriors in the snowy mountains to the south. He had been there six or seven days.

Westcott looked surprised. "Ask him if Black Horn led the raid on the wagon train."

Of the raid, the old Arapaho professed to know nothing, only that Black Horn and the Greasy Face warriors had come in with their spoils—rifles and whiskey and a few scalps—and then had gone away again.

"Ask him where they went," Westcott persisted.

They had ridden to where the sun sets, the old man replied.

"Ask him where did they go to hide from the bluecoats?"

Dunreath gave the old man a sliver of chewing tobacco, and then drew a rough circular map in the sand beside the log. He posed the question patiently, using the map to explain what he wanted.

The old man, however, said he did not know where the warriors had gone. He was too old for fighting or hunting, he explained, and the young Greasy Faces did not confide in him. But he added slyly that if he himself had done a bad thing against the bluecoats and was afraid to stand and fight them, he would ride west to the Porcupine country. In there, a warrior would be as hard for the bluecoats to reach as a star in the sky.

"He might be humbuggin' us," Dunreath said to Westcott. "Whether he is or not, we won't get any more from him."

Westcott pulled his hat on, his disordered red hair spraying out over his forehead. "They could be holed up less than ten miles from here. Better go look for tracks, Pete."

"A lot of tracks were headin' out of here—headed west like he said."

"Look for tracks in other directions," Westcott repeated curtly.

As Dunreath turned toward his horse, Sergeant Connors called to Westcott from the lower end of the village: "Sir, somethin' here the capt'n might ought to know about!"

Westcott squinted down the creek. "What is it, Sergeant?"

"We found a boy hidin' under some blankets."

Westcott frowned, and motioned Dunreath to wait. "Hustle him up here."

The boy, who might have been fifteen or sixteen years old, scurried like a flushed deer up the creek bank with Connors close behind. He was wearing a faded Army shirt and dirty brown Kentucky jeans.

When Connors halted him in front of the captain the boy glanced away, and Westcott wondered if his attempt at concealment indicated guilt or excessive fear. The youngster was handsome in spite of his mop of greased hair. Westcott thought there was something oddly familiar about the olive-skinned face. He was obviously a half-breed, and looked more Mexican than Indian.

Dunreath spoke sternly in Arapaho: "Why do you hide from the bluecoats like a shivering girl?"

The boy did not reply; his fingers played with a round object suspended from a chain about his neck, an amulet carved from a wooden beer case, the stamping of a bottle.

"He was with the warriors," Westcott guessed, slashing his hand down in anger. "He went with the warriors against the wagon train on Clear Creek!"

"I went only to guard the horses," the boy cried out in fair English, and fixed his handsome eyes defiantly on Westcott. Again there was something familiar about him.

"What are you called, boy?"

"John-day."

Westcott knew him then, with a flood of memories of Fort Laramie—five or six years back, while he was still a lieutenant at Laramie. The boy's name was Zha-day or some unpronounceable name that the soldiers had changed to John-day, spoken as one word, a bright-eyed little brat, always on the prowl around the fort with his grubby hands held out for coins to buy rock-sugar candy in the sutler's store. John-day's father could have been anybody. His mother was Arapaho, all right; she washed the enlisted men's clothing cheaper than the white laundresses, who had hated her for it. The officers in Old Bedlam had adopted John-day for a lucky talisman. They'd had him in to dance tribal dances on Saturday nights and showered him with pennies. That was before Westcott was ordered south under General Crook to help pacify the Apaches. That was before he went back East and met Anna Llewellyn at that West Point hop.

The boy was regarding him shyly.

"We were once good friends," Westcott said.

"Yes, Soldier-chief Westcott."

"You will talk straight to a friend."

"John-day always talk straight."

Westcott tried to hold the boy's eyes with his own. "Then tell me where the warriors are."

John-day glanced innocently up at Westcott, his dark eyes shifting to the leather pouch fastened at the captain's belt. Westcott got the meaning as quickly as if words had been spoken. He loosened the rawhide tie on his money pouch and pried a few coins out into his hand. "This sprout learned the value of money early," he said to Dunreath.

Dunreath nodded, grinning. "Nothing like a sutler's store to spoil a breed boy."

John-day already had his hands out, cupped, and then clutching eagerly at the coins that dropped from Westcott's fingers. The captain spoke harshly: "All right, tell me where they are."

"Black Horn and the Greasy Faces and some of the young braves of the Sagebrush men run away. They run away because trader with black hair on face is stronger than they. He make them go in fear." The boy held up his hands and made them quiver as with fear, the quivering spreading down into his body.

In Westcott's face now, there was eager alertness. "Who is this trader with the black beard? What do the white men call him?"

"The white men call him Yankee. He is strong and fears no one."

"Yankee—" Westcott repeated the name and swore. "Yaneka Snell!"

Snell had been at Laramie, too, Westcott remembered. A hunter who had a government contract for a while, and then a wood contract, but was too lazy to hold them. The commanding officer had him on the carpet once or twice for selling whiskey to the tribes, but was never able to prove a thing. Yaneka Snell, a heavyset man with a black greasy beard, large rolling protruding eyes, and giant hands. "Where is this man called Yankee?"

"He go with Black Horn and the braves—far to the Porcupines. You will never find him. He rides like the wind and is afraid of no man."

"How do I know you speak true?" Westcott shouted, catching at the boy's shoulders and shaking him roughly.

"I'll wager he's talkin' straight," Dunreath said, and spat tobacco juice in the sand.

Westcott drew another silver piece from his rawhide purse and flipped it to John-day. "We'll soon know if he's lied." He slapped the boy on the rump. "Go along, you little beggar." Westcott watched the boy jogging away up the creek, clutching the coins greedily in one hand. "Pete, you think the raid was Yaneka Snell's doing?"

"It explains why the paymaster's wagon got special attention, don't it?" Dunreath drawled.

"What would Black Horn and the Arapahoes get out of it?"

"Guns, horses—and whiskey from Snell. Except for that money-crazy John-day, the payroll wouldn't agitate the hostiles. It wouldn't be easy for them to spend greenbacks in this country."

Westcott slapped one hand against the holster at his waist. "I want Snell and I want Black Horn. The others don't matter."

"Sure," the scout said easily, "we'll find 'em." He drew a tobacco plug from his shirt pocket and appeared to be studying it carefully. "Ben, you're goin' to need more'n one troop to go into the Porcupines, with the hostile Sioux thick as they are in there."

"That's the hell of it." Westcott's voice was quiet, almost normal again. "I could ask for volunteers, but the whole troop would volunteer, you know it." He squinted at the sun. "If we move fast we can make it to Fort Wicked before dark. I can tie into the telegraph line there and ask for more cavalry." He paused as if debating his own thoughts. "Suppose Snell and Black Horn *didn't* go to the Porcupines?"

"I'd wager a month's pay they did."

"All the same, I want you to make a circle around this camp, looking hard for tracks. They *could* be—"

Dunreath gave him a lazy salute and turned toward his horse. As he crossed by the dying fire, he heard Westcott call an order to the corporal upstream: "Discharge your guard, Corporal, and let the Indians go about their business. Have your men give Sergeant Connors a hand with those rifles!" And his voice raised sharply as he shouted to the lieutenant on the slope: "Let the mounts wet their tongues now, Mr. Jackson! Reset saddles and have your troops ready to march in ten minutes!"

As he swung into his saddle, Dunreath glanced once more at the captain and sighed with audible relief. Maybe Ben Westcott was going to be all right again.

2

AS THE SUN DROPPED TOWARD THE SAND HILLS BEHIND C Troop, it lost its brightness, but heat was still on the land, the waves flowing into the men's faces and dancing on sandstone buttes ahead of them.

Captain Westcott kept the short column of twos moving doggedly, cutting the hourly rest stops to five minutes. The horses were too exhausted for changing pace to gallop or trot, and to ease the wear on them he gave frequent orders to dismount and walk.

During one of these walk marches, First Sergeant Mike Connors came up alongside Peter Dunreath. Westcott was several paces ahead of them, sweat marks dark across the shoulders of his blue shirt. "The capt'n's still pushin', but he don't seem so wild any more," Connors said.

"He's all right." Dunreath wiped a sleeve across his damp forehead. "If he wasn't all right we'd be headin' west for the Porcupines instead of to Fort Wicked."

"I'd like to know what he's thinkin' right now. I wager he's thinkin' what he'll do to old Yankee Snell and them Greasy Face Arapahoes when we come on to 'em."

Captain Westcott, however, was not thinking of Yaneka Snell or Black Horn. He was considering the Arapahoes back in the tepee village, the noncombatants, and wishing he had the power to put them on a reservation. That boy, John-day, the cowering squaws, and the old men—they'd all go hungry with half the warriors in flight and the others off with their chief trying to run deer out of the south mountains.

His thoughts drifted to his weariness, and he wondered how bone tired a man could be before he dropped in his tracks. He noticed varying patches of wild flowers on the flats to his left, waves of yellow, blue, and white. He'd never seen so many wild flowers in this country in June . . . must've been heavy rains in here during the spring. He'd given up trying to learn the names . . . remembered writing Anna about them, how everybody seemed to have a different name for Western wild flowers . . . when she came out she could set him right about them.

He pushed that remembrance away with all the others that had spun through his mind during the last three days—like the memory of her portrait and all the letters from her, and the faraway memory of holding her in his arms that last night at the Point. As he'd pushed thoughts of Black Horn and Yaneka Snell away until it was time to consider them again.

Over that farthest mottled ridge with its scattering of scrubby cedars lay Fort Wicked, or what was left of it—nothing but the telegraph line and Brad Carlin's trading post, and all the deserted old buildings. On one of the shelves of Carlin's store would be a bottle of Napoleon brandy, and he suddenly thirsted for it as he'd never thirsted for liquor before. He could feel its glow on his tongue and in his throat and belly—and the soft embracing forgetfulness of drunken sleep.

Ahead of the column the outriders had pulled in together, and that would be the juncture with the old trail. From there the marching would be easy. C Troop should make it in by dusk.

At the trail juncture, Westcott halted the men for five minutes. There was no talking, and little movement from the horses, and when he called the order to mount, they rode on with their shadows falling long before them, in silence but for the creaking of saddle leather and occasional jingling of harness metal.

By the time the troop reached the high point of the last ridge, the light was softer and the air a little cooler. Below, a small basin spread like a green oasis against the dull red buttes beyond. Hidden behind a screen of willows and cottonwoods was old Fort Wicked, and Brad Carlin's trading post.

As Westcott dropped his gaze back to the downsloping trail he saw the advance scouts slowing, and beyond them a covered wagon, headed the other way, halted in the middle of the road.

He urged his horse into a faster walk, motioning the column to keep closed up behind.

The wagon was old, green paint peeling from its wood, the canvas cover rotten and full of holes. The four-horse team, resting now, looked older than the wagon. From a slit in the rear canvas, Westcott saw eyes peering at him, and then as he turned his mount aside was startled to see a row of circular holes along the side of the canvas, a face in each of them. They were all young faces, children, of various ages.

A scraggly bearded man was crawling from underneath the wagon, a lanky, almost skeleton-like man, knotting a broken suspender as he slid out and crouched up on his haunches. He was answering a question put by one of the advance scouts. "Got a broke reach, soldier. Tryin' to hold it together with wire till I can move 'er down there to Benbow's Base."

"Benbow's Base?" the young trooper said, surprised. "Where's that, mister?"

"He means Fort Wicked," Westcott broke in. "The place used to be called Benbow's Base." He turned to the wagon driver. "Can we give you a hand?"

The man stood up, brushing dust from his sleeves. "I reckon you ain't carryin' no wire, are you, officer? That's all I need, a piece of wire. Seems like when a man wants—"

Westcott turned in his saddle. "Trooper, get down the column and find that signal corporal with the telegraph equipment. Bring him up here." He swung back to the wagon driver. "We can spare a few feet of wire."

As he dismounted beside the rear wheel and handed his reins to the other trooper, Westcott could feel eyes upon him from the holes in the wagon cover. He glanced up briefly, his face inches away from the head of a dark-haired girl, thrust outside the canvas. Her violet eyes, set wide apart, searching and hungry, looked into his as if she had known him all her life.

He turned away, disconcerted, wondering if she could be by some incomprehensible chance the wife of the scarecrow man in the trail. When he looked back again, that hole was empty, but other faces were still staring at him from the other openings.

Remembering his troop, he turned and shouted an order to Lieutenant Jackson to dismount the men. The signal corporal was coming up with the telegraph equipment.

"Go easy on that wire, Corporal," Westcott said. "Just enough to hold the broken reach."

The wagon driver wiped his hands on his greasy trousers. "Sure mighty obliged to you, officer." He stopped and peered after the two troopers who had crawled under the wagon. "I could fix it myself."

"How far've you come?" Westcott asked.

"South Pass, three days back. I'm goin' east. Got my bellyful of this country."

"See any Indians back there?"

"Once, yestiddy. Far off. Whole bunch, makin' tracks."

"Notice a white man with them?"

"Couldn't say, officer. Too far off. Glad they was, too."

"They heading west?"

He nodded. "North and west. Toward the range, I reckon."

Out the corner of his eye, Westcott caught a movement from the front of the wagon. A girl was there, half-standing, half-sitting on the seat, swinging one bare foot out over the front wheel. Her skirt was too small for her, and her legs showed above the knees, well-formed, like a woman's. Her tawny face came around the edge of the canvas, the same girl who had stared at him so earnestly from the hole in the canvas, and her eyes met his now in the same adult, knowing way.

"Julie!" the wagon driver shouted, scolding. "I told you all to stay in there. If'n you come out, t'other young-uns want to come out. Now git back in there 'fore I lay my whip 'cross your back!"

The girl vanished.

With a sniff, the wagon driver added: "Them young-uns sometime give me a mite of trouble." He dug at the hairs in his nose. "Wife died a time back."

"How many in your family?" Westcott asked politely.

"Nine. All females."

Westcott whistled. He could feel the muscles relax in his face, and realized he'd smiled for the first time in three days. "Nine girls," he said. That would be something to tell Dunreath.

He told Dunreath about the nine girls as they rode down the slope toward Brad Carlin's trading post. Behind them the column split into two files, passing the slow-moving wagon as it rattled along the trail, the weary troopers coming to life momentarily as they passed in turn the tattered canvas and saw children's faces staring at them from the holes.

Before cutting in toward the creek where the troop would camp for the night, Westcott glanced back up the hill. The wagon looked chocolate brown against the washed-out blue sky of twilight.

"Nine female young-uns," Dunreath said. "Whoo-ee. You see all kinds on this old trail, Ben. Some headin' west, hopeful. Some headin' east, dead beat." He yawned. "Here's a dead beat one, hisself, Captain. Gonna get me a bottle of Brad Carlin's Injun whiskey and lie right down in the grass with it."

Westcott thought of the Napoleon brandy on Carlin's liquor shelf, but there were other things to be done first. He had to get that telegraph tied into the line and persuade the Yellowhorse command to spare at least two cavalry companies for the pursuit into the Porcupines.

*   *   *

The western horizon was still light when Westcott finished his exchange of telegraph messages with the commanding officer at Fort Yellowhorse. Two understrength cavalry troops would leave Fort Kinney at dawn under command of a major, to rendezvous with Westcott's C Troop at the South Fork of the Bittercreek tomorrow night. Westcott did not like the thought of relinquishing command of the pursuit to a major unknown to him, but at least he was making progress. And the Bittercreek rendezvous was close enough to allow a leisurely departure on the morrow, giving his horses time to regain their strength. C Troop could march out by noon and be at Bittercreek before the two companies from Fort Kinney arrived there.

His last act before walking over to Brad Carlin's trading post was to instruct Sergeant Connors to collect cold rations from among the men and take them to the covered wagon which had drawn up below the cavalry bivouac. A campfire was already glowing over there, but he suspected the scarecrow father of the nine girls was short on rations. He remembered the hungry look on the girl Julie's face when she looked at him from the hole in the canvas.

As he walked up the sand-margined creek, frogs were beginning to chatter in the marsh. Brad Carlin's trading post lay just ahead, overshadowed by a deserted commissary building loom-

ing in the dusk behind it. Carlin's store was constructed like a
redoubt, with rotted sand-filled gunny sacks packed around its
logs. The store had been the first building in the basin, and the
original owner had come to stay, designing it as a miniature
fortification with crude bastions, flanks, and a roof parapet.

Above the entrance, an ancient wooden sign swung gently in
the wind, its letters crudely carved: *FORT WICKED.* No one
could remember who first used that name, but at one time the
description was apt. Originally the place was known to travelers
as Tipsword's Ranch; then when the Army came to build its
huge supply base there, it was changed to Benbow's Base in
honor of the quartermaster colonel in charge of construction.
But somewhere along in its earlier years, an anonymous trapper
or trader had labeled it Fort Wicked, and though the name
never appeared on any map, it was used more often than
Benbow's Base, even in official communications. This very
night, Westcott recalled, he had given his location by telegraph
as Fort Wicked, and no one had questioned it.

Fort Wicked! Two years ago he'd been in winter quarters
here, and recalled how he had marveled at its warehouses, harness shops, cook and bunk houses, wagon sheds, stables and
corrals. More than a hundred wagon and pack trains operated
from the depot, and never were there less than a thousand
mules in the corral. A company of infantry and three hundred
civilians—teamsters, packers, laborers—had manned the place,
the largest supply base in the West, designed to serve twelve
Army posts, some as far away as four hundred miles. It had
been built at enormous expense of lumber and bricks freighted
overland—in anticipation of the coming of a railroad. When the
railroad was routed sixty miles to the south, Benbow's Base, or
Fort Wicked, was doomed. A new base was constructed at
Newcomb's Wells on the rail line, and Fort Wicked's buildings
now lay deserted and empty along the slope back of Carlin's
trading post.

In the thickening dusk, Westcott stood there under the sign,
with the feel of the wind cool against his damp shirt. His desire
for brandy fought with his reluctance to face Brad and Maude
Carlin. He would have to talk about *that,* and right now he
wanted to nurse a bottle until stupor destroyed his thoughts and
enclosed him in a drunken sleep.

A yellow light flamed suddenly inside, rousing him to action. He pulled at the leather door handle, causing a bell to jingle, and as he stepped inside he faced Brad Carlin in the act of setting an oil lamp down upon the counter. Carlin's head was centered in the ring of light, a stout, ruddy-faced man, neatly shaven, his long sideburns graying a little.

"What the hell kept you so long, Ben?" Carlin asked gruffly, and turned his back on the captain. He banged at a catch on a heavy wire screen that protected his shelves of liquor, lifted the frame with an exaggerated grunt, and selected a bottle. The brandy was the most expensive liquor in his stock, and when he held it up to the lamplight the glass showed about three-quarters full. He blew at the dust on the bottle, then finished wiping it away with his shirt sleeve. "I can tell when you're about due in here, Ben, by the thickness of dust on this bottle."

"Don't tell me nobody else dares drink that stuff." In spite of his effort at lightheartedness, Westcott's voice betrayed his weariness.

"You know damn well none of my other customers can afford it—besides it's got your name on it." He lifted a small drinking glass from under the counter.

"Don't bother with a glass," Westcott said. "Unless you want to join me." He stepped across the creaking floor boards, picked up the bottle and drank until the burning in his throat forced him to put it down again. He loosed the yellow scarf from around his neck and wiped his face, sniffing the odors in the crowded trading room—leather and tobacco, new cloth, old smoke.

"You'd better sit down," Carlin said. "You look like a peaked owl. Hollows under the eyes."

Westcott took the bottle and moved over to a chair by a stone fireplace, remembering suddenly that the last time he had sat there a fire was blazing and snow was falling outside. The chair was a willow frame made by Brad Carlin; his wife Maude had covered it with a strip of faded carpet cloth, sewing in a doeskin pillow at the top. Westcott removed his hat, set the bottle carefully on the floor, and eased into the chair. His lean knees jack-knifed up in front of him, but there was something satisfying about the chair, and he said so to Carlin.

"A good seat to get drunk in," the trader agreed. "A man

can't fall out of it." He polished the counter top briskly with a
rag, ignoring his visitor until Westcott finished a second draw
on the brandy bottle. "Pete Dunreath was up here while ago,"
Carlin said then. "He told mc about it."

Westcott ran a hand through his disarranged red hair, his
face tightening. "Brad—"

Carlin cut him off: "You want to talk about it, I'll listen."

"You heard it from Dunreath, didn't you?" Westcott's voice
had a raw edge to it. He picked up the brandy bottle again.

"All right." Carlin turned and shouted back through a green
calico curtain into the living quarters behind the store room, his
gruff voice suddenly louder: "Maude!" He repeated the call,
holding a hand up against Westcott's protest. "She's got to have
her say, now Ben," he insisted gently. "You know women. Soon
as she's said it, she'll git. Then we can pow-wow. I got a lot on
my mind."

Maude Carlin appeared suddenly through the curtain, her
face lighting up when she saw Westcott in the chair. "Captain
Ben," she cried, and hurried around the end of the counter, her
full skirts rustling. Westcott arose and they shook hands.
Maude was a large woman, older than her husband, but as
everybody said, a physical match any day for Brad Carlin. She
acted as an equal partner in the trading store, lifting heavy bags
and boxes like a man, and the only softness in her was her
regard for Brad Carlin—and sometimes for Ben Westcott.

Maude held Westcott's hand now in a tight grasp, her bright
eyes shining as she studied his face, and then she said: "It was
the Lord's will, Ben Westcott."

Westcott nodded stiffly, dreading what she might say next,
and was surprised when she asked: "You had your supper?"

When he told her he had, she shook her head dubiously,
looked him up and down, and commented sharply to her husband: "Army grub don't stick to a man's ribs any more, does it,
Brad? Whyn't you go out and kill one of your spring chickens
right this minute for Captain Westcott?"

Westcott protested firmly that he was not hungry. He wanted
only the brandy, he declared, and Brad came to his rescue:
"When a man's drinking, he don't want victuals, Maude."

"All right, I'll hush," she promised, "if he'll come for breakfast."

"I'll be honored," Westcott replied quickly, "to sit at your table for breakfast."

Maude smiled at him, and touched his wrist. He glanced down awkwardly at the blue-veined, toil-worn hand against his, and wished to God he could tell her how he felt.

After she had gone for a minute, and Westcott was settled back into the chair, Carlin fumbled two cigars from a box under the counter. He lighted both of them from the oil lamp, and took one around the counter to Westcott.

"I'll smoke your weed," the captain said, "if you'll share a drink of this brandy."

"You know I never touch the stuff." With a forced sigh, Brad lifted himself upon the counter and began swinging his moccasined feet back and forth. He puffed out a blue cloud of smoke. "What you figgering to do now, Ben?"

"Go after the runagates, of course. I want you to pack me six days' rations for sixty-three men. And some oats for the horses."

"You didn't say when."

"By eleven o'clock in the morning."

"That's better. I don't have any hankering to stay up all night with that ornery sergeant of yours watching me pack. Specially since the quartermaster never paid me yet for the last rations I packed for C Troop."

Westcott rolled a swallow of brandy around his tongue before he replied. "Maybe the QM got a smell of that dried beef you passed off on us last time." A trace of a smile brushed briefly across his lips.

"Ah, now." Brad swung one leg up on the counter, and leaned back against a stack of meal bags. "C Troop wouldn't never know good beef from bad."

Neither said anything more for several minutes. Westcott removed his cavalry boots. Smoke thickened in the room, and the level in the brandy bottle dropped lower. Brad stretched and yawned and stared at the ceiling. "That Arapaho band, Wolf Moccasin's," he observed soberly, "ought to been put on a reservation. Trouble wouldn't never happened, had they been."

"Why don't you write a letter to Washington?" Westcott replied bitterly.

"They'd pay more notice to a letter from you," the trader shot back. "You, an Army officer."

"I already wrote a letter. Washington advised me that Wolf Moccasin's band belongs at Wind River with the Shoshoni."

Carlin sat up and made a quiet but profane comment of one word. "Like asking a cat to lie down with a dog. Any fool knows Wolf Moccasin's band's been enemies with the Shoshoni long as anybody can remember. They'd ought to have a place they can live in some pride."

Westcott nodded absently, his head drooping a little. A gratifying peacefulness was beginning to spread through his body. "You'd make a good Indian agent, Brad. You keep liquor to sell, but you don't drink it, and you never sold any to an Indian."

"How you know I never sold liquor to an Indian?"

"The Army knows."

"Well, it's not just because I got a noble heart," the trader said stubbornly. "I just want to keep my hair on."

Westcott stiffened suddenly, harshness coming back into his face. He closed his eyes but could not shut out the grim memory of the ringleted scalp drying on the hoop back in the Arapaho village. He shuddered, groping for the bottle on the floor, drained it, and tossed it into the blackened fireplace.

Brad Carlin frowned, knowing he'd said the wrong thing. He changed the subject with studied casualness: "I noticed you brought company in with you this evening. That wagon. But I ain't seen a peep of 'em. Seems like you'd least have the decency to bring in travelers who're hankering to swap their money for my goods."

Westcott opened his eyes, found difficulty in focusing them. "You won't get any trade out of that wagon driver," he said thickly. "Poor devil likely hasn't got two bits entire."

"Dead beat, heading East, I'll bet."

"Widower, with nine daughters."

"Christ all mighty. What's he aiming to do with all of 'em?"

"Ask him. That's one problem, at least, the Army isn't concerned with." Westcott nodded sleepily, his voice dying away, his arm hanging limply to the floor.

The trader yawned deliberately. "Reckon it's time to crawl in the shucks. I'll put a pallet down for you back there in the pantry."

Westcott managed to shake his head negatively. "I like this chair better."

Brad slid off behind the counter, his moccasins slapping on the creaky floor as he went back for a blanket. When he returned and dropped the cover over Westcott, the captain was asleep. It was the first time Westcott had lost consciousness since he'd heard the news at Sun River of the attack on the wagon train.

3

WHEN WESTCOTT AWOKE, GRAY LIGHT WAS FILTERING through the barred window behind him. During the night the blanket had slipped to the floor, and his muscles were cramped and stiff. The other pain—deep inside him—began again, dulled a little by time, and he realized then that time eventually would distill that memory almost entirely.

But his hatred for Yaneka Snell and the Arapaho, Black Horn, was still bitter within him, and as he got into his boots, stamping his feet down into them, he felt a surge of impatience to begin the hunt, an eagerness to be in motion.

He slipped the bar lock on the front door, reached up and held the clapper of the bell with one hand, and eased the door open. Gray dawn filled the basin, and birds were already beginning to sing. The first thing he looked for was the covered wagon, half-concealed in haze along the creek. As he walked down the trail to where his troop was bivouacked, the brassy sound of a reveille trumpet shattered the morning air.

When Westcott reached the camp, Lieutenant Jackson and Sergeant Connors were crawling out of their blankets. The scout, Dunreath, still lay with his head covered against the sunrise, snoring off his night's drunkenness.

Westcott ordered the lieutenant to have men and horses ready for inspection at eight o'clock. "Any horse or trooper unfit for hard duty will remain behind. A farrier detail will be needed to replace worn shoes up at Carlin's smithery. We'll be marching out at eleven o'clock."

The lieutenant saluted, and Westcott turned to his saddlebag. He removed soap, razor, a muslin towel, a spare shirt, and his uniform frock coat, and walked down to the creek. He washed his face in the cold water and began working his razor carefully over his sprouting red beard, removing only enough stubble to make himself presentable. *Presentable for whom?* he wondered suddenly. Maude Carlin was accustomed to seeing bristle-bearded officers—on patrol across alkali flats where a clean-shaven face was an invitation to misery. He realized with annoyance that he'd been watching the wagon for signs of activity, and had been thinking of his appearance in relation to that tawny-faced, hoyden daughter of the scarecrow wagon driver. He swore under his breath, cleaned his razor in the stream, and wiped his face dry. The sun was just breaking over the piny ridge to the east.

He looked spruce and refreshed as he came up to the rear of Carlin's store, crossing the weed-grown parade where an ancient brass warpiece and a disarranged stack of cannon balls marked the site of the vanished flagpole. He passed a shed where the Carlin's milk cow and a mule looked out dubiously at him, then a flourishing vegetable garden, and along one side of the deserted commissary building, a fenced chicken run filled with busily scratching hens. As he came up to the rear door of the trading store, pleasant aromas of coffee and bacon drifted out to meet him.

Brad was sitting at a long table just inside the door, packing rations for C Troop. "Christ all mighty, Maude," the trader cried in mock astonishment, "here comes a parade-ground soldier! You better go put on that new bustle."

Like all Maude Carlin's meals, the breakfast seemed to Westcott even better than the last one he had enjoyed there: fresh scrambled eggs, biscuits, bacon and coffee, trout, and as a special treat some fresh radishes from Brad's garden.

At last they pushed their chairs back, Carlin and Westcott lighting up stogies while Maude cleared the dishes. "I'm dead serious, Brad," Westcott said. "You're wasting your time here, and the Indian Bureau's losing a good man who ought to be a reservation agent. You understand the Indians, you could teach them farming, livestock raising. Why don't you let me put your name up?"

"I like it right here," Brad said. "No papers to fill out, no reports to make, no politicians to toady to. I like it the way it is."

"But last night, you said yourself—"

The ringing of the front bell alarm interrupted Westcott. "Likely that's one of my troopers," he said, shaking his head in irritation as he got up and followed the trader out through the curtains to the store room.

But it was not one of C Troop's men at the door, it was the lanky wagon driver. He stood hesitantly on the outer threshold, holding the door open with one bony arm. He removed his dusty slouch hat, and nodded his balding head apologetically. "Mornin'," he said to Brad, and repeated the greeting to Westcott, who walked on around the counter and stood by the fireplace. "Things changes hereabouts, ain't they?" the man continued. "I come in here figgerin' to find work."

Brad leaned over the counter, studying the man. "You won't find any work here, stranger. Fort Wicked's deader'n a petrified skunk."

The man shook his head. "Three years back on my way to South Pass, I stopped off here a few weeks and earned good pay. Why, they was hundreds of men workin' here them days, wagons a-comin' and a-goin', soldiers and Irishers all over the place. Big Indian village right down there where my wagon's a-settin'."

"That's all gone now," Brad said. "Army closed out the supply base."

The man sucked in his hollow cheeks. "I *got* to find work, mister. Got to buy somethin' to feed my family 'fore we can go on." His eyes followed the row of foodstuffs on the shelves, fixed on the hams hanging from a rafter, then turned to Westcott. "Thanks to your kindly soldiers, officer, we had good grub last night, but I swear to you both, I'm cleaned out."

Westcott said awkwardly: "I can spare enough to hold you a day or so. If I gave you more, my tail would be in a sling."

"I surely do appreciate that." He turned back to Brad, blinking solemnly. "You wouldn't sell me a barrel of flour on trust, would you now, mister?"

"Look, stranger, I see lots like you. Folks never should've come out here in the first place." Brad's voice turned gruff: "Maybe the captain don't see so many—he can afford to give it out once in a while."

"I'll send you the money," the man pleaded, almost whining. "Soon's I get to Kearney and work it out."

Brad slapped the counter with the flat of his hand. "Go outside and look around. There's nothing left here but my place, of all Fort Wicked. My trading store was here before the Army come in. It'll be here till hell freezes over or they lay me under. But not if I trust anybody but me, any living soul but me, you understand?"

"Mr. Carlin means it," Westcott said bluntly. "I've known that tight-fisted trader for eight years and he wouldn't let me have a drink of water before he saw the color of his money."

"Now wait a minute," Brad said. "I'm always open to a swap. You must have something you can swap for a barrel of flour."

The man's eyes seemed to be reading the shelves again, the bottles, cans, and boxes, the sacks of meal on the counter, the two sealed flour barrels at the far end of the room, the hams hanging from the beams. His boney fingers twisted at his hat. "You got any children, mister?" he asked suddenly.

"Why, no—"

The man's lip curled, like a harried dog's, over his long teeth. "Well, I got nine. My wife died and left me nine daughters. What good to a man are nine daughters?" He backed toward the door, the bell jangling as he jerked on the catch. "I'll be right back. Make you a good swap."

He was gone before Brad could say a word. Westcott took a last long draw on his stogie and dropped it in the fireplace. "He's got you across a barrel, Brad. Right across a flour barrel."

"It's things like this," Brad muttered in disgust, "make me want to change my mind about staying a trader."

A few minutes later the man was back, driving his ancient wagon up the trail from the creek. Westcott had delayed his departure, curious as to what the swap offer would be, and what Brad's reaction would be, and he was waiting with Carlin in the trading room when the jangling bell announced the return of the wagon driver.

A girl came in first, the one with the curious violet eyes. She was wearing the same calico skirt that was too small for her, and a man's light flannel shirt with numerous patches on it, her small unconfined breasts rounded against the rough cloth. Behind her was the father, pushing her inside, his eyes shifting from Brad to Westcott and back to the trader again. The girl held her hands tightly clasped, watching Westcott and following his gaze down to her bare feet.

"Well, here she is, mister."

"What you driving at?" Brad asked suspiciously.

"I said I'd make you a good swap. One of my daughters for a barrel of your flour."

Brad forced a grin. "Now, I can take a joke, mister, but I got work to do, packing for the captain's troop."

"I ain't jokin'," the man replied stubbornly.

Brad's mouth opened, but he could find no words to speak.

"You said you got no children. This one'll be a help and a comfort to you." He added hastily: "Course I'll send for her soon's I'm able."

He'll never be able, Westcott thought. The girl was paying no attention to Carlin or her father, keeping her steady gaze on the captain as if she and Westcott were the only persons in the room.

"You mean it right enough, don't you?" Brad said then.

"She's the pick o' the lot."

She's probably the biggest troublemaker, Westcott thought. *More than he can manage with the other eight besides.* The girl was still looking at him out of those long-lidded dark eyes, as if she shared some secret with him.

"Her name's Julie," the father said pridefully, and he pushed back her tousled hair from her forehead and ears so that it fell in disorder over her shoulders. "She'd be right purty if she was fixed up."

"Maude!" Brad turned and shouted: "Maude, come out here!"

Maude came out, drying her hands on her apron, her eyes bright as she listened to Brad's explanation of the man's offer. Maude Carlin was of a more resilient nature than her husband, and she had lived too long at Fort Wicked to be surprised by anything. She took the stranger's story at face value, only her shining eyes betraying her excitement. "Of course we'll keep the little girl for the poor man," she said firmly. "It's the Christian thing to do, Brad." She put an arm around the girl, who glanced up only briefly at her and then looked back to Westcott.

The wagon driver pressed his bargain: "You'll throw in one of them hams, ma'am?"

"Of course," Maude replied, "a ham, and you'll need lard, salt, and saleratus. See to it, Brad."

"Don't need salt, ma'am. Take some sugar instead. The little girls like sugar."

With the look of a man who believed nothing of what he heard or saw, Brad Carlin came around the counter and mechanically lifted a ham down from a rafter. Westcott helped him roll a flour barrel to the door, and the three men lifted it into the rear of the crowded wagon. From the holes along the sides of the canvas, the remaining eight daughters watched the proceedings with grave curiosity.

Maude and the girl Julie stood just outside the door under the Fort Wicked signboard, the woman with a protective arm still around the girl's shoulders. Julie's expression did not change, not even when her father climbed into the driver's seat and called down to her: "Be a good girl now, Julie. I'll send back for you."

He picked up the lines, all his actions speeded up as if fearful that Brad would realize he had been swindled in the swap and might call the whole thing off. He thanked the Carlins loudly for their kindliness, and slapped his emaciated team into motion. The wagon creaked and rolled forward, picking up speed on the slight downgrade.

I'll bet he never even repaired that wire-patched reach, Westcott thought, and looked back at Julie. *And she knows she'll never hear from him again.*

She was shading her eyes with her hand, watching the wagon turn down toward the main trail through a grove of cottonwoods yellow-green in the first sunlight of morning, watching the only home she knew disappearing into its own dust.

Brad walked in front of the girl, deliberately cutting off her view, wondering what he could do to comfort her. "In a few days he'll send back for you," he said reassuringly.

"No, he won't. He won't." The girl's voice was husky, betraying her dry eyes, and Westcott realized they were the first words he'd heard her speak.

She turned suddenly, pulling away from Maude, looking up at the wooden sign that rocked gently in the early breeze. "Why do you call this place Fort Wicked?" she asked.

Brad laughed, bent down facing her, and gripped her shoulders. "You can read then, girl?"

"Ma taught me. 'Fore she died. She taught me to read from the Holy Bible. She made me read her a verse every day."

"Now, ain't that wonderful, Brad?" Maude was smiling with pleasure. "Julie, girl," she said brightly, "we're going inside and have us a bite of peppermint candy. Then we'll give you a good bath and put some new clothes on you."

"Yes'm." She pulled away from Maude's hand and looked back to Westcott as if to communicate to him some secret message of leavetaking.

When the door closed, Brad said: "I believe she's kind of taken a shine to you, Ben."

"She's a little coquette," Westcott replied.

Brad thrust his hands in his pants pockets and began walking back and forth. "I reckon Maude's going to be as busy as a hen with one chick." He grinned suddenly. "Her first name's Julie," he said, "but you know, by God, that skinny wagon driver never even told me the family name."

"It'll be Julie Carlin, won't it?" Westcott looked away toward his cavalry camp, the old feeling of bleakness surging up inside him again. For an instant he had been caught in the swirl of others' misfortunes, and had almost forgotten the bitter purpose which had been driving him.

As if reading his thoughts, Brad said: "I better get back to packing rations."

Westcott turned to start back toward his camp, then reconsidered. "Before I go, I want to thank Maude for that breakfast —and incidentally see how she's making out being a mother."

As they went through the store room into the kitchen they could hear water splashing in the pantry beyond, and Maude's low reassuring voice. The pantry door was open, and like conspirators the two men trod lightly across the kitchen floor until they could see inside.

Julie was sitting in a washtub, her back to them, and Maude was down on her knees industriously soaping the girl's shoulders. As the washcloth pressed into the small of her back, Julie winced, but she did not protest even when Maude picked up a kettle and rinsed the soapsuds away with steaming water.

"That feel good, Julie?" Maude asked softly.

"Yes'm. It tickles."

Maude laughed to herself, and then began tying the girl's wet hair up in a ponytail, knotting a string to hold it in place. "We'll find us a bright red ribbon out in the store for this pretty hair. Now, you just hold still while I work over these pink ears." Julie squirmed and pulled away with a splash, but she made no verbal complaint.

"Wasn't a bit bad, was it? Now you stand up, child, and we'll be done with this bath in three shakes of a sheep's tail."

Julie stood up gingerly in the tub, the soapy water streaming down her firm rounded legs. She turned as she rose, and when her eyes met Westcott's watching from the pantry door, she showed no surprise or embarrassment, only her lips breaking in a secretive smile. Her thin body was pink from the scrubbing, her auburn hair gleamed under its sheen of wetness, the tightly pulled ponytail revealing the delicate feminine lines of her neck.

Westcott's face turned as red as his hair, and when he caught at Brad's arm to draw him away from the door, Maude noticed them for the first time. "Saints to goodness!" she shouted. "How long you two been standing there peeping in?" She stood between them and the girl, apron spread, hands on hips. "You got things to learn around here, Brad Carlin, such as a young lady's bath is supposed to be private." She turned on Westcott then: "And I'm surprised at you, too, Captain Ben, you supposed to be an officer and a gentleman. Now, you two prowling tomcats—git!"

As Maude moved toward the door, Westcott could not resist one more glance at the girl. Julie's smile had widened over a row of perfect white teeth. She was still looking at him, completely unashamed, making no effort to hide her proud nakedness, when Maude slammed the door shut with a loud bang.

Brad was shaking with silent laughter. "Like a mother wolf!" he whispered hoarsely, and dug an elbow into the captain's side. "Like a mother wolf, by God!"

"Captain Westcott, Captain Westcott, sir!" a voice was calling from outside the kitchen door.

Westcott swung around. One of his troopers was there, saluting as the captain appeared in the doorway. "Sir, Lieutenant Jackson begs to inform the captain the troop is prepared for inspection."

* * *

At eleven o'clock sharp, C Troop was ready to march. The inspection turned up no ailing troopers or mounts, and the farrier detail had taken care of the worn shoes. Brad Carlin's six-day ration packs and a small supply of oats for each horse were stowed away in saddlebags.

As was their custom, Brad and Maude had come down to the creek to bid farewell to their favorite cavalry troop, and this time there was a third member of the party—Julie, arrayed in a light red-checked dress that fell almost to her ankles. She was also sporting a bright red bow of ribbon in her ponytailed hair, and a pair of beaded moccasins from Brad's choicest stock of women's footwear.

Westcott's face was solemn as he shook hands with Brad, and all the trader's efforts to put his friend into a lighthearted frame of mind were ineffectual. When the captain kissed Maude's cheek lightly, she whispered: "Take care, Ben," and patted his shoulder.

"Goodbye, Julie," Westcott said, and bent down and brushed her cheek with his lips. To his surprise, the girl locked her arms around his neck, and she held on so tightly that he had to pull away by force. When her eyes suddenly filled with tears, he turned away abruptly, taking his bridle from his orderly. He mounted, guiding his horse in at the head of the column, where Peter Dunreath and Sergeant Connors were waiting.

"Order the men to mount, Sergeant!" Westcott said sharply.

"Hold on a minute!" Dunreath's head came up warningly as he shouted, and Westcott turned quickly in his saddle. Julie was standing right behind his horse; she had followed him up from the creek.

"Move away, girl," he said gently.

"I want to go with you." She came around to the side of the horse, putting one hand against Westcott's boot. Her dark violet eyes were still wet.

Maude was hurrying after her up the sandy margin of the creek. "You go on back with Maude," Westcott ordered.

"I can ride pillion behind your saddle," she insisted, wiping a streak of tears away from one cheek with the back of her hand, "I won't make you no trouble."

"Julie, Julie." He shook his head slowly, waiting for Maude to come. "Be a good girl now."

Maude took her arm, scolding her quietly.

Sergeant Connors bawled the order to mount. Leather creaked, and carbines rattled in unison in the slings.

Westcott raised a gauntleted hand. "For'ard!" The march began slowly under the hot June sun.

Connors settled in his saddle, and winked over at Dunreath. "Looks like the capt'n made hisself a friend back there."

"She's a game little pullet," the scout commented. He could feel the sun already burning whiskey out of his pores.

Westcott looked back only once. Julie stood in the sand, apart from Maude and Brad, a small and lonely figure in an attitude of mute accusation. He swung around to the front, and the fresh memory of Julie faded into the brutal face of Yaneka Snell dancing like an evil vision against the copper-colored buttes ahead.

4

EACH MORNING WHEN JULIE WAKED IN THE NARROW LITTLE
bed that Brad had built for her in the pantry, she would dress
hurriedly, rush out the back door, and walk up the slope to the
old brown commissary building so that she might have a clear
view of the north basin. It was in that direction that Captain
Westcott had marched away with his cavalrymen, and it was
from there that she expected he would return.

On the sixth morning after C Troop's departure, she went
through the same routine, hurrying past the mule shed, crossing
a deep dry ditch, and then stopping, almost breathless, at the
end of the old building. Her eyes followed the crooking trail
along the green-fringed creek until it disappeared among a row
of reddish buttes far to the northwest. But no dust showed
anywhere to mark the movement of approaching horsemen. She
sighed, and turned toward the pine-studded ridge behind which
the sun would rise in a matter of minutes. She liked that ridge
best of all, with its ranks of dark lodgepole pines that seemed to
be marching down like soldiers into the basin.

This morning Julie was carrying an old rag doll made of flour
sacking, a doll four feet tall with black buttons sewed on to
represent eyes, nose, and mouth. She had found it on a curtained shelf in the Carlins' bedroom, and Maude was delighted
when Julie asked if she might play with it. "Take it for your
own," Maude said. "It once belonged to a little girl who grew
too big for dolls."

"Am I too big for dolls?" Julie asked.

"A girl is not too big for dolls until the boys come courtin'
her," Maude replied with a laugh.

Julie gave her a curious look. "I'll keep it until Captain Westcott returns," she said.

She had learned to make imaginary conversations with the doll, carrying it about carelessly in one hand, gripped so tightly around the middle that its sacking had split up one side, and she had to keep packing the cotton stuffing back inside. During the past few days she had explored, in company with the doll, all the old buildings of the base except two—the dull-hued commissary and the stone guardhouse. Brad had forbade her ever to go beyond the bounds of the fort, and had also warned her that snakes sometimes wandered into the old guardhouse dugout and into the cellar of the commissary.

This morning, however, she decided she would be brave enough to talk through the forbidden commissary. After a quick look over her shoulder to make certain that neither Brad nor Maude was out back watching her, she skipped up the dilapidated steps and stood in the entranceway of the long building. The old door sagged on its hinges. All the glass was gone from the rows of windows—taken away by the Army when the base was abandoned—and twittering birds were darting in and out.

The wooden flooring, warped from exposure to weather, creaked underfoot, but she crossed it, bracing her courage with a few words to the doll until she came to a stairway that led to the cellar. Here she hesitated, torn between curiosity and fear, gradually transferring her own misgivings to the doll, first reassuring, then scolding it for being so cowardly. Clutching the doll tight against her breast, she went deliberately down the steps.

Dimly lit by rusted iron-barred ventilators, the cellar was cool and dry, with faint odors reminiscent of fruits and vegetables once stored there. Julie peered into the darker corners, searching for snakes, but saw nothing more terrifying than a few wasps and spiders. A half-dozen empty colored bottles on a recessed shelf intrigued her. She swung the doll in one hand and picked up one of the bottles, holding it to the light, admiring its delicate greenness, wondering if she might take some of them back to the house. But she knew that Brad would guess where they came from, and then he'd scold her for going down into the cellar.

Yet, if she left them there, she thought, something might happen to them, someone might take them away. She looked about for a hiding place, but the cellar seemed bare of nooks and crannies. She noticed then that the lower shelf board was loose. She lifted it, and found a dark hollow in the stonework below it, laced with spider webs. In a minute she had stowed all the bottles carefully into the cavity, and replaced the shelf. Then with a sigh of satisfaction, she took up the doll and turned back toward the stairs.

When Julie came out of the commissary, she saw Brad sitting on the kitchen stoop, but he had his head down honing a butcher knife for Maude and did not notice her. In a soft voice, she warned the doll not to breath a word to anyone of their shared secret, especially the hiding place of the colored bottles.

She took a deep breath of the winy breeze coming down off the pine slope, and then, almost unconsciously, looked to the north again. The whole upper basin was in bright sunlight now, the trail like a twisted brown ribbon beside the green of the creek. She saw the dust cloud then, faint but unmistakable, and the tiny figure of the lead horseman.

She jumped high, her skirt flaring, her moccasins padding the earth as she came down. She rushed down the slope toward the kitchen door, her ponytailed hair flying behind her. "Brad!" she cried. "They're coming back!"

"Who's coming back?" Brad asked, his eyes blinking against the sunshine.

"Captain Ben Westcott, that's who, with his horse soldiers."

"And now how did you come by this fine piece of news?" Brad held up the butcher knife, testing the edge lightly with his thumb.

"I *saw* them. They're coming from that way." She pointed to the north, rocking on her heels and swinging the doll.

He stood up and entered the kitchen leisurely, dropping the knife on the table. "Julie says somebody's coming down the north trail," he said to Maude. "I'll go and have a look."

"Don't stay too long." Maude was busy over the stove. "Bacon and eggs be ready in ten minutes."

Brad went out, and took the girl's hand and they walked up toward the end of the commissary building, Julie tugging impatiently at his fingers, her feet almost dancing. As they reached the crest of the slope, he saw the dust, closer now, and the riders, only five of them.

"They're not all there," Julie said, her voice thin and disappointed.

"And they're not soldiers," Brad replied. His eyes squinted, studying the riders. At least some of them were Indians, he knew from the swinging of their stirrup-free legs. "Probably a bunch of bucks off a reservation, Shoshoni maybe, coming in to trade skins. I hope they've got better stuff than I took in last week."

Julie was leaning against him, disappointment crushing her gay spirits. "Sorry to dash your hopes, Julie, girl." He lifted her chin with a finger. "Come on, let's see that fine smile again. Cap'n Ben will be riding back in here any day now." He squeezed her shoulders. "Let's go down to breakfast."

5

AS BRAD CARLIN HAD GUESSED, FOUR OF THE RIDERS AP-
proaching Fort Wicked were Indians, but they were not Shoshoni, they were Arapahoes, and the fifth rider was a white man
wearing heavy boots set securely into his stirrups. He was a
large man with a dark overgrown beard that hung almost to the
saddle pommel. His saddlebag contained more than five thousand dollars in greenbacks, and in a small pouch hidden inside
his buckskin shirt was another thousand dollars in gold eagles
and double eagles. The rider was Yaneka Snell.

Snell was mounted on a bright-blooded bay with jet-black
mane, tail, and forelock. He had stolen the animal two days ago
after shooting its owner, a rancher. In the fight the rancher
managed to kill two Arapahoes, which Snell considered no loss,
as his main objective at the moment was to be rid of the other
four, one of whom was Black Horn, the arrogant subchief of the
Greasy Faces.

Three days ago Snell had decided to separate from the Arapaho raiding party and head east into Nebraska, with a vague
plan of drifting down to the Kansas cow towns where he could
find women, gambling tables, and good liquor—and properly
enjoy the large fortune that so easily had come his way.

From the time he left the Arapaho village with Black Horn
and the renegade Greasy Faces, he had felt a growing distaste at
the thought of spending the summer hiding out in the
Porcupines. In there, his money would be useless; the only sport
would be hunting, the only women a few Sioux squaws jealously
guarded by the tribe's warriors, and no whiskey trader was
anywhere near.

Snell was rather certain that the Army could not have connected him with the raid on the wagon train. He had been careful to remain out of sight until the Arapahoes routed the escort patrol; then he had galloped in quickly, shot the wounded paymaster dead, and hurried away with the stolen sack of money. His principal regret was that he had not kept riding straight eastward. Another thing that bothered him was the preponderance of greenbacks in the payroll sack. He knew that any man showing too many greenbacks in this Territory would be viewed with suspicion. Only soldiers were paid with Treasury notes, and when they traded them at the post sutlers' the sutlers usually shipped the paper back East for goods as quickly as possible. Snell had secretly transferred the thousand dollars in gold eagles and double eagles to his inside pocket for immediate needs; the greenbacks would have to wait until he traveled into Kansas or farther east.

It was while the Arapaho warriors were breaking camp to begin the last day's ride through the passes into the Porcupines, that Snell made up his mind to leave them. He mounted and rode up to Black Horn and made the subchief an elaborate farewell speech.

Black Horn listened politely, then expressed his displeasure in blunt Arapaho fashion. He had been disappointed, he said, in the small quantity of whiskey obtained in the raid. It was true that his warriors had captured a few fine horses and some guns. It was true he had been lucky enough to take for himself the scalp of a white woman, and he was now wearing on his chest a shiny neckpiece that had belonged to her. But he was thirsty for white man's whiskey. In the bag carried by the black-bearded one, was there not gold that would buy whiskey?

At this question Snell calmly opened the bag and showed Black Horn a packet of paper notes. "It is only green paper," he said. "The traders will not give whiskey for green paper."

With an angry gesture, the subchief dashed the paper money from Snell's hand. "Why does the hairy-faced one guard it so well if it is worthless?" he demanded.

Snell's pale eyes swelled with anger, but he contained his feelings and got down from his mount to retrieve the money. He patiently explained to Black Horn that only white traders far to the east would give whiskey for the green paper. That is why, he said, he wanted to leave the Arapahoes and go toward the rising sun.

Black Horn pondered for a moment, then slyly replied that he would go with his friend, the black-bearded one called Yankee. They would ride together toward the rising sun where men were so foolish as to trade whiskey for green paper. Nothing Snell could say would dissuade the subchief. Black Horn selected five of his favored warriors to make the journey with him. The others of the raiding party would ride on into the Porcupines where the white man's pony soldiers could never find them.

Snell's first plan was to keep his word, ride rapidly eastward all the way across the line into Nebraska, and at the first trading post he would buy a quantity of whiskey—using the secreted gold if necessary. Then he would turn the liquor over to Black Horn, and as soon as the Arapahoes were deep in drunkenness, he would make his break for Kansas.

But a series of unforeseen incidents forced Snell to change his plan. During the afternoon of the first day's journey, his horse went lame. One of the hoofs developed a sand crack, so bad that the break spread each time the horse's weight fell upon it. He would have to find another mount.

Not far to the south, he recalled, were a few scattered ranches, most of them well fortified, but he decided the odds would be in his favor with six armed Arapahoes in his company. He told Black Horn what he planned to do, and turned the party southward. At dusk they sighted a low ranch building back in a draw. It was constructed of logs, with small loopholes for windows. The corral lay next to the ranch house, as close as a back yard. He held the Arapahoes in an ash thicket until dark, and then they rode in silently.

Snell almost succeeded in stealing a horse without incident, but some slight sound must have alarmed the owner. The rancher came out the rear door with a rifle, and the fight was on, in the starlight. Two of the Arapahoes foolishly rushed in to take a scalp; they did not live long enough to reach the ranch house. Snell downed the rancher with his Sharps buffalo rifle, but fire raked the raiders from the fortress-like building, and he barely got away with his saddle from the lame horse.

They rode until midnight, and after he settled down beside a sinkhole with the surviving four Arapahoes, he began to make new plans. He knew that by morning an alarm would be out, through the sparsely settled grazing country. His best chance was to move south rapidly, all the way to the railroad and board the first train that came along. California or Kansas, what was the difference? Either place offered safety and the pleasures that could be purchased with his stolen moneys.

Before he could do that, however, he had to be rid of Black Horn and the others. He thought of killing them as they slept, but rejected the idea as being too risky. Then he remembered Fort Wicked, and Brad Carlin's trading store. Carlin kept a liquor stock. A long day's ride and they would be at Fort Wicked. There he could purchase enough whiskey to put the Arapahoes out of action, and he could be halfway to the railroad before they were sober again.

At the first sign of daylight, he started them for Fort Wicked. They failed to make the distance the first day, largely because he insisted upon taking a circuitous route over terrain that left no easily detected tracks for pursuers.

But now, this morning, Fort Wicked was in sight. Snell made a cautious approach, alert for smoke from cooking fires along the creek that would reveal the presence of soldiers. He was relieved to find no evidence of any patrols or anybody else in the vicinity. He halted once, studying the main trail running east and west across the south basin. No dust showed in either direction for five miles or more.

Confident that Brad and Maude Carlin where alone, he led the Arapahoes in at a brisk pace. He avoided the short cut across the weed-grown parade of the old fort, following instead the sandy trail along the creek.

In the screen of cottonwoods he halted and told Black Horn to wait there with the other three warriors.

Black Horn shook his head. "Want whisk' now!" The stolen locket that had belonged to Anna Llewellyn swung back and forth across his naked chest.

"White trader not sell whiskey to Indians," Snell replied impatiently. "Yankee go buy whiskey. Bring here."

"Want whisk' now," Black Horn repeated stubbornly. "Go with Yankee."

Snell's wide flat fingers rested on the butt of his revolver, his eyes bulging with anger. "Black Horn, stay here!"

The subchief jerked his pony back, watching the white man slyly. Once again Snell remembered the gold inside his shirt and the greenbacks in the saddlebag. He had come too far to lose it all now. He swallowed his anger. After all, what could Carlin do against five? "All right," he said. "But Yankee will make all talk with trader. We don't want trouble."

Black Horn, knowing he had beaten a white man with words, slapped his quirt triumphantly and started his pony at a gallop toward the trading store. Snell swore, and spurred the bay after him. The hoofs of five mounts drummed as they dashed up the side trail toward the front of Carlin's store.

The sudden onset of noise brought Brad out the front door, hatless and unarmed. Maude and Julie, also surprised and curious, followed a moment later. Maude was not alarmed. She had seen Indians ride in like that before, racing, full of high spirits. But she noticed Brad was frowning. He was studying the huge figure leaning over the bay, a white man with a streaming black beard. Brad was not sure until the man raised his head; then he knew.

He made a fatal error then, and he knew too late that he erred, and tried to stop his motion as he plunged toward the door of his store. The scream of a bullet brought him to a standstill. He turned and saw Snell standing in his stirrups, his buffalo rifle up.

"Yankee Snell!" Maude cried, and caught Julie, pushing her back toward the door. The rifle cracked again, lead spanging into the wooden sign above her head.

Snell was already out of the saddle, walking toward them, his rifle at ready. "What you feared of, Maude?" he asked, his loose lips grinning mirthlessly through his beard. He stared hard at the girl. "Don't remember that one." He looked around warily, his head held high. "Anybody else here?"

"That's for you to find out," Brad said bitterly.

"Don't give me no sharp tongue. Why'd you make that move, Brad?"

"You know why, you—" He cut off the profane phrase. "Maude, you and Julie get inside."

"No they don't!" Snell said warningly. He shouted back to

the Indians: "One of you bastards tie my horse." He spoke in crude Arapaho to Black Horn, who still sat on his blowing pony, and ordered him to send one of his braves inside the store to look around.

As the Arapahoes grasped the meaning of what was happening, they drew their rifles—all new ones stolen from the wagon train—and dismounted, hitching their mounts with Snell's to the tie-rail. One of them, at Black Horn's command, entered the store, his head jerking up at the jingle of the bell.

Black Horn moved over beside Snell, arrogant and menacing as he pointed his rifle at the Carlins, the gold locket flashing back and forth across his naked chest.

"Just stand easy, Brad, you and Maude," Snell said. "Black Horn's awful quick with a trigger."

Brad moved in front of Julie. "What you want, Yankee?"

"I want to know why you tried to make a run for your gun when you saw me comin'."

Brad's anger at himself had cooled; he wanted to reassure Snell, make him think he knew nothing of his connection with the attack on the wagon train. "All I saw was a cloud of dust and a bunch of wild bucks riding down on my place," he replied calmly. "If you'd been me, Yankee, you'd wanted a gun, I guess."

"I guess." Snell spat, and his blunt broken-nailed fingers tightened over the rifle barrel. "Except I'd never be caught without a gun." He laughed, his red lips showing through his heavy beard.

The bell jingled over the door again, and the brave who had gone inside came out, a scarlet blanket flung across one shoulder. His shrug and outspread arms told Snell the place was empty.

Brad's eyes narrowed when he saw the blanket. "You come in here to steal me out, Yankee?"

Snell looked indignant. "Who said he stole that blanket?"

"You want to trade, put your guns away," Brad said mildly.

Snell laughed again. "Not now we don't." He turned and spoke in Arapaho to Black Horn. The subchief nodded and started for the store entrance. "You all follow Black Horn inside. He'll keep you covered in there, so you better not make any sudden moves, none of you. I'll be right behind."

They entered the trading room, single file behind Black Horn, Brad first, then Julie and Maude. Snell kept his distance, his eyes swelling as he came into the contrasting shadows. He kicked the door wide open and shoved a small keg against it to hold it, and beckoned the other three Arapahoes inside. With his rifle, he motioned the Carlins to move over by the fireplace.

"I generally wait on my customers," Brad said.

Black Horn had set his rifle against the counter and was fingering balls of hard candy out of a glass jar. The other Arapahoes went over to share in the spoils.

"Don't know why they so crazy 'bout that sweet stuff," Snell commented. "What *I* want's a good long pull of old red rye."

Brad smiled crookedly. "You want me to serve you?"

"You stay where you're at," the big man said, and lifted himself onto the counter, still holding his rifle steady on the Carlins. He swung his heavy boots up and slid over, the rifle scarcely changing position. A glance at the liquor shelves told him the wire cover was locked. "You don't trust nobody, do you, Carlin? Everything locked up." He frowned angrily at Black Horn, motioning to the Indian's rifle leaning carelessly against the counter. "Keep them covered!" he said, repeating the order in Arapaho. Black Horn crushed a candy ball noisily in his jaws as he lifted his rifle.

Snell kicked one of his heavy boots against the lock on the wooden frame. When it failed to snap, he smashed at the wood.

"You got no cause to do that, Mr. Snell," Maude protested. "Brad will give you the key."

He ignored her plea, searching around until he found a hatchet under the counter, and pounded the lock until it sprang open. He raised up, grinning at Maude. "Never seen no lock yet I need a key for." He swung the screen up, and took out an armful of bottles.

Black Horn's eyes gleamed. "Whisk'! Whisk'!" he cried. He swung his rifle around carelessly, but as he did so Snell grabbed his own weapon from the counter. "Carlin!" The bottles rolled on the floor, two of them breaking, and the raw smell of whiskey filled the room. Brad's muscles relaxed; he had been ready to dive toward the end of the counter, where he kept a shotgun concealed in a spring clip under the top boards.

"Next time you look at me like that, Carlin, I'll shoot," Snell growled. "And you, you whiskey-crazy Arapaho—" With a foul oath, he ended his tongue-lashing of Black Horn, took another bottle from the shelf and snapped its neck off cleanly against the counter edge. He poured the liquor into a tin cup and shoved it toward Black Horn, who grabbed it up and sucked greedily.

Somewhat more leisurely he opened four more bottles, supplying the three Arapaho braves with one each, and then ordered them outside to sit in the shade and keep a sharp watch on the trail approaches.

He swung his thick buttocks up on the counter again, facing the Carlins. He laid his rifle across his knees and took a short swallow from his bottle. He smacked his red lips and wiped the spilling from his beard.

Then he spoke suddenly, his voice booming in the crowded room: "Maude, what you heard about me makes you so skittish? What you know about me, old Yankee Snell?"

Maude gave him a prim look. Her patience was wearing thin. Her feet were planted firmly on the hearthstone, one hand pushing Julie back behind her skirts. "All I know about you, Mr. Snell, is what folks been saying for a long time now. Not much for a white man to be proud of."

Snell took another pull on the bottle. "They say anything *special* about me, recent-like?"

Maude lifted her chin. "I don't listen to gossip, Mr. Snell. Too busy."

"Well, now." He grunted, cocked his head sidewise, peering at Julie's tawny face thrust out behind Maude's defiant bosom. The girl's violet eyes watched him with fearful fascination. "Who's she?" he demanded. "The little filly there?"

As she answered, Maude fought a sudden quaver in her voice: "We're just keeping her for a time, that's all."

"You ever hear of me, gal, old Yaneka Snell?" When Julie's head disappeared behind Maude, he slammed the bottle on the counter. "Don't be a-feared of old Yankee. Come out here, gal, come 'ere!" He slapped his leg with a flat-fingered hand as if he were summoning a dog.

"You leave her be," Brad broke in angrily. "She's got nothing to do with it."

Snell slid off the counter. "When I say come, you come, gal, hear me?"

Julie glanced at Brad. She knew that Brad was about to do something that would endanger all of them. She knew she had better do what the big man said. She flung herself forward and around Maude, avoiding the woman's suddenly outstretched hands, and looked back to Brad as if to warn him to hold still. She stopped in the middle of the floor, facing the black-bearded man. She was still clutching the ludicrous button-faced doll.

"There now's a gal with fire." Snell leaned against the counter, his rifle resting in the crook of his arm, his eyes moving up and down over her figure. "Ain't you a mite big to be playing with dolls?"

She shook her head.

"I asked you if you ever heard tell of me."

She looked straight into his pale blue eyes. "I've heard."

"What do folks say about me, old Yaneka Snell?"

Her fingers dug into the ripped seam along the doll's side. "Captain Ben Westcott is looking for you, that's what," she said firmly.

Snell leaned forward, his black beard outthrust, the Sharps tight in his hands. "Westcott!" he shouted, and threw a savage look at Brad. He moved toward Julie, his boots heavy on the creaking floor. "And what would that redheaded horse soldier want of Yaneka Snell?"

Julie took one step away from him, afraid of his rolling eyes and his whiskey smell. "She was his sweetheart, the girl with the wagon train, Miss Anna Llewellyn," she replied quietly.

Snell's forehead wrinkled, his jaw working loosely. "The girl from the wagon train?" He swung around toward Black Horn who was squatted on the floor, sipping at the liquor in the tin cup. "You son of a bitch! You done that." His voice was a snarl. "And you had to go and take her scalp." Black Horn raised his head; he knew the black-bearded man was angry, but he did not understand the words he was using.

Frightened now, and angry, the big man turned his wrath on Brad, mouthing incoherent curses until his throat turned dry. He backed to the counter, picked up the bottle of rye, holding it to the light, squinting in surprise when he saw how much of it he had consumed. He set the bottle down without drinking, his forehead still furrowed. He didn't like the way Brad Carlin was watching him. He'd have to stay cold sober to figure his way out of this. So the Army knew; they always found out sooner or later. And it would have to be that Westcott who was after him, that stubborn redheaded bastard—hard enough he would be to shake, even without that scalped girl mixed up in the deal. *So she'd been Westcott's sweetheart! Christ, the captain would be crazy for revenge.*

His swollen eyes shifted to Black Horn squatted down the counter, and he wanted to kick the bloody devil, tear that stolen locket off him, cut his savage throat. But that would not be the way.

He would have to kill the Carlins and that girl, too, stop all their tongues. He could do it easy—one, two, three—with the Sharps. Maybe it would be better to let the Indians kill them. No, they'd want scalps, and the way they were acting, especially Black Horn, they could just as well turn on him in any sudden flare of violence against the three whites. His fingers curled against the trigger.

But even if he did the shooting, the Indians would go blood crazy, and he could never kill the three whites and Black Horn, too, and hope to get past the other warriors out there.

In desperation, he caught up the bottle, wetting his throat with a short swallow. Julie shifted her position slightly, and his eyes fixed on her. She was a juicy little piece, full of fire, almost a woman. He blinked suddenly. Why not use her? He grinned to himself, pleased at how easily the plan formed in his mind.

"Black Horn!" He edged down the counter, nudging the Arapaho up from the floor, and catching at the rope's end from a reel set into the floor. "Knife," he grunted in Arapaho, and showed Black Horn where to cut the rope. "We tie up trader and white squaw," he explained. The Indian weaved uncertainly in his moccasins as he followed Snell toward the fireplace. Julie drew back against the window grill, her eyes widening with fear.

Brad casually drew out his watch, flipping the battered lid back. "It's past eleven, Snell," he said.

Snell stopped, his bloodshot eyes suspicious, muttering. "Tie him up, Black Horn." Black Horn grabbed for Brad's swinging watch, snatched it triumphantly, and held it to his ear.

"The stage from the East," Brad added, "always gets in here before noon."

Snell moved sideways toward the barred window, his boots scraping on the floor. Julie crouched away from him against the wall. From the window, he could see only part way down the side trail. The three Arapahoes were not in sight.

He turned around. Black Horn was still playing with the watch.

"Put the rope on him!" Snell's voice was almost a scream. His outflung hand came down on Julie's head, and he gripped her hair in his fingers. "I'm takin' the little filly with me, Brad, hear me?" He squeezed the struggling girl tight against him. "Tyin' you and Maude up, and takin' her with me. And if you let out so much as a peep to anybody on that stagecoach, or you come after me, you won't see this little gal alive again. You keep your mouth shut, Brad, and I'll let her go in two days, I swear."

"You always did talk mighty big, Snell." Brad kicked the rope away from his legs, ignoring Black Horn's threatening gestures.

Julie, still struggling, scratched suddenly at Snell's neck. He cursed, and brought his hand down over the stretched calico across her buttocks, and squeezed. She whimpered in pain, then drove her fist into his lower belly. The instant that Snell's rifle was flung up, Brad dived across the floor.

Although Brad's momentum brought his outstretched fingers to Snell's boots, the big man side-stepped, smashing Julie into the wall, and stamping down on one of Brad's hands. A second later Black Horn landed on Brad's back. The trader struggled to his feet, a wild man, his good hand going for the Indian's throat, catching in the stolen locket's chain and snapping it. The gold case spun across the floor to where Julie was crouched. She picked it up and used it as a weapon, beating ineffectually at Snell's knees.

With a final effort, Brad tried to swing Black Horn off his back against Snell, but his strength failed him. Braced against the wall, with no chance to fire, Snell used the Sharps as a club. He struck Brad a glancing blow on the shoulder, and as the trader stumbled, the rifle barrel came down again with a hollow crushing sound of metal against flesh and bone. The unconscious trader and the half-drunken Indian sprawled at Snell's feet.

As the black-bearded man's head came up, his mouth open and gasping for breath, he remembered Maude, and his blood-shot eyes blinked at the fireplace. The woman was not there.

"Drop your rifle, Mr. Snell!" Maude said hoarsely. "At once." She was behind the counter, with a shotgun leveled at Snell's belly. When he hesitated, her tone sharpened: "I can put a ten-inch hole in you at this range, Mr. Snell!"

With his left hand he dropped the Sharps back against the wall; with his right he reached for his revolver. In the instant of will that brought her to press the trigger, Maude saw Julie crouching close to the wall behind the big man, and in that instant she shifted her aim so that the explosion drove the center of the charge into the wall on the right. Had she not done this Snell would have been a dead man; as it was, he was hit with scatter shot in the leg above the knee. His left leg buckled, and he dropped on that knee, cursing as blood stained into the greasy cloth above his boot top.

Shaken by the gun's recoil, Maude remembered too late to reload. Snell drew his revolver, took deliberate aim, and fired. The bullet struck her in the chest. She coughed softly, her arms and head sagging to the counter, almost in an attitude of prayer, then as her legs crumpled, she slid out of sight.

Julie screamed, putting her hands over her face. An instant later, the three Indians who had been stationed outside crowded in the open front door. They jabbered excitedly in Arapaho, waving their liquor bottles and rifles. One pointed excitedly down toward the east trail.

Black Horn, still squatting on the floor, had his knife out, his whiskey-heavy eyes fixed speculatively upon Brad's scalp. But something urgent in the braves' voices brought him to his feet. He weaved toward the door, looking off toward the east.

In a matter of seconds, the Indians were gone, their guttural monosyllables drowned out by the sounds of their horses' hoof-beats as they swung around the trading store and turned back toward the north.

None of this was lost on Snell. He groaned and cursed alter-nately, half-crawling, half-walking to the door. The rocking stagecoach and its curl of dust, not two miles away, was no surprise. But he was surprised to see his horse still there at the hitching rack. The Arapahoes, he thought, had been too frightened or too drunk to take along the bay in their precipitate flight.

As he turned around to face the girl, still huddled under the window, he was startled by the trail of his own blood across the floor. He stumbled toward her, punched at her shoulder with the muzzle of the Sharps. When she refused to budge, he caught at her ponytailed hair so hard that the skin of her forehead stretched tight and her eyes filled involuntarily with tears. "Move, you little bitch!"

He half-dragged her out of the building, cursing to himself as he felt his blood trickling into his boot. The stagecoach had disappeared behind a roll in the basin floor, and he could see only the faint streamer of its rapidly approaching dust. He jabbed the Sharps into its boot, and slapped the girl across the mouth, fighting her until he got her up in the front of his saddle, her calico skirt ripping along a seam to her hip. She screamed Brad's name, leaning forward over the bay's black mane, the doll still clutched in one hand. Her teeth chattered over the sound of Brad's name.

As Snell untied the bay, he yelled at her to shut up, then mounted, pain shooting into his groin. He looked down at his blood-soaked leg and knew that unless he stopped the flow he could not ride far.

He spurred the bay into rapid motion, holding Julie and the reins tightly, and rode around the store. When they came up to the overgrown parade, he could see the Arapahoes galloping wildly away toward the north.

He slowed his horse, studying the deserted buildings carefully, then turned toward the more distant limestone guardhouse on the left. He glanced back once; the trading store screened him from the approaching stagecoach. With a grunt of satisfaction he guided the bay around the stone building, dropped down a sharp bank, and halted. The guardhouse had been built above a dry creek run to take advantage of the land's slope so that a basement floor could be added with a minimum of excavation. The rear entrance was a heavy oaken door.

After a futile attempt to open the door from his saddle, Snell dismounted. It was all he could manage, even with his powerful arms, to slide the door back on its ancient rollers. As soon as the opening was wide enough, he led the horse and the girl inside and pulled the door shut. There was no inner lock, but he was confident the girl would not be able to move the heavy oaken frame.

The lower floor of the guardhouse was dimly illuminated and poorly ventilated by a series of small grilled windows along the upper wall facing the fort's parade. A wooden bench ran along the earthen floor beneath the grills, and rusted iron rings once used for confining prisoners still dangled from the supports.

With a groan of pain, Snell stumbled toward the bench. The bay side-stepped skittishly, backing down toward the end of the dugout. As soon as the horse stopped its motion, Julie carefully dismounted, the doll hugged to her breast, and ran past Snell to a stairway that led to the upper floor.

The big man lifted his rifle, watching the girl as she moved up the steps. She pushed frantically at the heavy wooden trap door, first with her hands, then with her back. Snell ordered her to come down, holding the Sharps steady on her until she had done so. Then he dragged himself up the stairway and tested the trap until he made certain it was either barred or nailed shut. "You see, gal, there ain't no way out."

She had climbed upon the wooden bench and was on tiptoes, peering through one of the spider-webbed window grills. Her eyes followed the dust marking of the stagecoach's course until it turned off the main trail and began the slower approach into Fort Wicked. She drew in her breath, waiting expectantly, and as soon as she saw the lead stage team pull beyond the edge of the trading store and halt there, she cupped her hands and screamed with all her might.

She heard Snell's curse and sensed his movement behind her, but she screamed once more before his heavy hand dragged her from the bench and flung her to the earthen floor. The fall knocked the breath from her, and she lay gasping from the pain and shock.

She watched Snell sit down on the bench. He removed his boot, and with his knife cut the trousers leg above the shot wounds. Little streams of blood oozed down his naked leg until he used strips of the cloth to bind a tourniquet. "If you let out

one more peep, gal," he said without looking at her, "I'll have
to kill you."

Knowing he meant it, she lay where she had fallen, her arm
around the doll, one ear against the cool earth floor. She knew
Brad was alive. She had seen the slow movement of his breathing just before the black-bearded man had forced her to leave
the trading room and mount his horse. She wondered where
Captain Westcott was. If Captain Westcott was following Snell,
he would find him, and when Captain Westcott found Snell he
would find her. She decided that she would do what the black-
bearded man told her to do—until Captain Westcott or Brad
came near enough to hear a cry for help.

From far down by the trading store came the faint whinny of
a horse. Snell lifted himself on the bench and looked out one of
the gratings. Julie sat up, listening carefully for voices or other
sounds, but she could hear only the hoarse breathing of the
bearded man. When she pulled the doll into her lap, she felt a
hard round object through the cloth of her dress pocket. It was
the gold locket that Brad had torn from the Indian's neck and
sent spinning across the floor. She could not remember putting
it in her pocket. She held it higher into a beam of sunlight
falling through one of the ventilators, and the dancing reflection
brought Snell's head around in a quick jerk. "What you got
there?"

She did not know what to call it. "A fancy piece," she replied, watching the locket spin on its broken chain.

Snell grinned at her through his beard. "Black Horn's gee-
gaw," he said, and lowered himself to the bench. "You like
purty things, gal?"

"Yes, sir," she said quietly.

His eyes glistened as he looked at her. "You stick with old
Yaneka. He'll buy you lots of gee-gaws. Come here, and sit by
old Yaneka."

She kept her position, cross-legged on the hard-packed dirt
floor, looking away from him.

He leaned the Sharps on the bench and moved toward her,
his fat-fingered hands reaching out, but she jumped up and
moved back toward the restless horse in the rear. He grimaced
with sudden pain, slapped disgustedly at his leg, and hobbled
back to the bench.

"Don't be a-feared of me, gal." He muttered to himself for a moment, retightening the tourniquet, and then lifted both legs to the bench. After placing the Sharps alongside the wall, he stretched out beside it with his head resting in his enormous hands.

Time dragged away. Julie returned to the center of the room. She was afraid there might be snakes back in the darkened area where the horse stamped restlessly. She sat down and watched Snell until his eyelids drooped, then she tiptoed to the bench and climbed up, looking out over the wind-driven grass.

Straight across the parade, by the old fort's burying ground, she saw a small group of men, six or seven, and she wanted to scream again for help. But she guessed they would not hear her, and she was sure Snell would be angry enough to kill her if she tried that again. One of the men had a white cloth wrapped around his head, and when he moved she knew that he was Brad. Two of the men were digging in the ground, and after a while all of them took their hats off and stood in a sort of semicircle. Brad and the two men with shovels picked up something wrapped in gray blankets, and she knew they were burying Maude Carlin. She remembered her own mother being buried like that by two tall men with their hats in their hands, all strangers, and she whispered to herself a little prayer the preacher-man had read that day.

When the burial was over, the men turned toward the trading store, disappearing one by one behind the brown commissary building. Brad was the last one, looking back over his shoulder at the grave.

A few minutes later she saw one of the men again—he was the stage driver—out in front of the lead horses, checking harnesses fastenings. Not long afterward the horses began moving and the stagecoach circled the turn-around. As it turned, she saw Brad's bandaged head in one of the windows, then the coach was gone again. Her throat tightened and began to ache. Brad was going away, leaving her all alone with the black-bearded man! She almost cried out, but remembered Snell's threat, and choked the sound away.

She dropped down from the bench, moving listlessly back to the center of the room, and sat cross-legged, her eyes filling with tears.

As the afternoon wore on, Snell grew more restless, his leg paining him, and once he sat up on the bench and began digging at one of the deeper wounds with a sharp-pointed knife. He pried a small bit of shot out, releasing a gush of blood. Tightening the bandage, he talked and swore to himself, ignoring the girl who sat quietly holding her doll and watching daylight grow fainter in the windows.

About dusk she heard a whispering sound in one of the ventilators, and a black snake dropped down upon the bench, uncoiled, and slithered across the floor. She jumped to her feet, screaming, and Snell rose up, hand on revolver. When she pointed at the snake, he drew down to fire, but shoved the weapon back in its holster. "Blacksnake won't hurt you," he growled. The reptile crawled across the floor and disappeared through a crack under the heavy door.

Snell pulled himself up and looked across the parade ground. Night was falling and there was no movement outside, no sign of a light anywhere. "I could've shot it and nobody'd heard. That stage went on long ago." He turned back to Julie. "If I could trust you, gal, I'd send you down there for some whiskey and grub. But you wouldn't come back, would you?"

She had moved back beside the horse, and was almost invisible in the dying light.

"No matter," he said, and sat down with a loud groan. "We'll move out of here 'bout midnight."

Outside the sun had dropped behind the basin rim, and darkness thickened in the guardhouse room. The girl moved away from the horse and sat down on the floor again. She could not see the black-bearded man, but she could hear his heavy breathing, and after a time he began calling her. He got off the bench and prowled in the darkness, cursing first the girl and then his leg, but when he came near her, she would slip away quietly so that he could not hear her movement. In the end his wounded leg defeated him, and he floundered back to the bench. She heard the scrape of his rifle and the clatter of his single boot when he stretched out. For a while he muttered to himself, and then there was only his hoarse breathing.

She fought against sleep, standing until weariness drove her to sit down. The bay, restless under its saddle, stamped about in the lower end of the dugout, its sudden noises keeping her awake for a time, and then in spite of her will, she lay down and fell asleep.

When she awoke, pale light showed in the ventilators. Snell was stretched on the bench, mumbling in a fevered sleep. She rose and moved slowly toward the door, watching the man's bearded face as she gripped the wooden handle and struggled to free the heavy oaken frame. Snell's eyes opened and focused upon her. "You ain't goin' nowhere, gal, not without old Yaneka." When he tried to sit up, his voice turned to a moan of anguish, and he squeezed at the flesh above his wound. The lower part of his leg was swollen and inflamed. "Time we got out of here, gal." He tried to stand, but the leg would not support him, the pain torturing him.

Julie stood with her back against the door, her hands pressed to the heavy boards, watching him.

After a while, he looked up at her, his tongue licking at his lips. "See here, gal, you and me, we got to make a bargain. You can't get out without me to crawl over there and pull that door back. And you got no place to go without me, hear? Old Yaneka can buy you a thousand fancy gee-gaws, anything you want, you go with me, anything you want." He patted his shirt where the gold lay hidden, drew out a handful of the shiny metal pieces. "You go over there now to that horse and bring me my saddlebag. I'll show you something real nice."

She kept her place by the door, watching him. His eyes were enormous, and he kept talking, his voice high and feverish. "Go on now, bring me that saddlebag!"

Her eyes never leaving him, she moved close to the bay and hauled down the saddlebag. It had a crudely designed wing-spread eagle cut into its cover. When she approached Snell, she kept her distance, shoving the bag across the floor to his feet.

His flat fingers moved over the fastenings. He drew out a stack of green Treasury notes, his eyes bright and protruded as he grinned at her. "See it, gal! Look here, a fortune just for you and me!"

She still kept her distance, watching him as she had watched the black snake crawl across the floor. He stuffed the notes back into the bag. "Now, you'll go with Yaneka, won't you!"

Again she was silent, and her silence angered him. He strapped the bag shut. "Put it back." She waited for him to

shove it toward her. Instead he put his hand on his revolver
butt. "Pick the bag up and put it back, I said." His voice turned
hard and threatening.

She hesitated a moment, and then as she snatched for the
leather straps, he lunged at her. But she was too quick for him,
spinning away, her torn skirt swirling. He stumbled upon his
good knee, swearing violently.

"We gittin' out of here, now!" He climbed awkwardly upon
the bench, looking out the window, and his sharp cry of mingled pain and surprise told her he had seen something outside.
She hung the bag over the bay's saddlehorn and climbed up to
the ventilator farthest away from him.

A dozen mounted men were gathered around the empty corral behind the trading store. At first she thought they might be
soldiers and was disappointed when she saw that none wore a
uniform. Nor did she recognize Brad among them.

"Damn ranchers," Snell muttered, and warned her sharply
not to cry out.

She watched the ranchers for a long time. The men smoked
and talked in leisurely fashion, then one of them seemed to be
giving orders. They rode out in little bands of two and three,
heading in different directions.

Like most searching parties, the ranchers overlooked the ob-
vious, and rode in wide circles around the basin, searching for
horse tracks or other sign.

At midday the stagecoach, bound east, made its run, omitting
its usual Fort Wicked rest stop.

Through the afternoon, Snell and the girl—he ignored her
presence most of the time—kept a close watch on the activities
around the trading post, she hoping the men would begin a
search of the buildings, he cursing them for their stubborn thor-
oughness.

Late in the afternoon, a band of clouds formed in the west,
spreading gradually across the sky. The horsemen ended their
circling, and formed into two groups, one heading north, the
other west along the main trail. After they were gone, Snell sat
down heavily upon the bench, his fingers squeezing continually
into the upper flesh of his leg. The reddish swelling had spread.
He was hot with fever, and mumbled to himself for minutes at a

time. Once he fixed his eyes upon Julie, glowering, as he promised her they would go when it was dark.

But when darkness fell—the dusk came early because of the
cloud cover—he still lay stretched upon the bench, mumbling
crazily with fever and pain. As she had done the night before,
Julie took her place in the middle of the floor.

For the first time her fear was giving way before demands of
thirst and hunger. She closed her eyes and imagined she could
see clear cold water running in the creek.

Restless for water and irritated by the saddle still upon its
back, the horse pawed and snorted behind her, and when the
animal quieted she heard Snell snoring, a harsh rattling vibra-
tion from his open mouth. She waited patiently for ten or fifteen
minutes, then after carefully placing her doll on the floor, she
got up and moved back to the bay, caressing its forehead and
shoulder.

In the darkness she found a coil of rope below the saddlebag.
She climbed into a stirrup and began fastening one end of the
rope securely to the saddle horn. After this was done, she led
the horse slowly toward the door, and fastened the other rope
end to the wooden door handle.

She waited in the blackness, listening to Snell's feverish rattle,
and then crept back toward the room's center, crawling about
on hands and knees until she found her doll. Behind her the bay
moved impatiently, feeling the tug of the rope and beginning to
paw at the hard earth. Snell moaned, and shifted his position.
She heard the scrape of his rifle stock, and held her breath until
his snoring began again, quieter and more rhythmic.

Her first plan had been to strike the bay across the rump with
the doll so that it would lunge forward and pull the door open.
But she could not bring the fidgety animal into the proper position. She climbed into the saddle, with the rope tight against
one of her thighs, and brought the reins down sharply against
its shoulders. As the horse pulled forward, the rope burned into
her leg, the door creaked, and then the bay turned sideways,
fighting the tension on its saddle.

Aroused by the noise, Snell thrashed about on the bench,
grumbling loudly, his words unintelligible. Julie's teeth bit into
her lip as she held the bay steady. She could not feel the rope
against her thigh any more, and when she dropped one hand to

the saddle horn, the rope was gone. Snell was still mumbling in his feverish half-consciousness.

She turned the horse slowly about, guiding it toward the door. Under the starless sky, the darkness outside was almost as black as the inside of the guardhouse, and she could not determine whether the door had been opened until she came up to it and dismounted. The opening was less than a foot wide. She would have to leave the horse.

She edged toward the opening, but the bay blocked her passage, standing with its nose in the aperture sniffing the damp night wind. She shoved against its shoulder, and as the animal moved her fingers touched Snell's saddlebag. Before the horse backed away she pulled the bag down, and clutching it and the doll in front of her, she slipped out the narrow opening and began running.

She ran straight for the trading post, stumbling and falling, picking herself up and falling again a dozen times before the black shape of the store formed out of the night. The door was barred and locked. For a while she stood listening, but there was no sound other than the rising wind. She scurried around the building and found her way to the sheds. Inside the open shelters she could make out the vague forms of the milk cow and the mule, but Brad's riding horse was gone. Opening the crib door, she climbed over a heap of grain sacks and began burrowing a hollow into the loose hay. She stowed Snell's saddlebag and her doll deep down, then pulled the sweet-smelling straw over her, and in spite of hunger and thirst drifted into sleep.

Big drops of rain beating on the sheet-iron roof woke her in a nightmare of terror in which she dreamed Snell was squeezing her with his enormous hands. She squirmed up out of the hay and saw lines of gray light marking the cracks in the crib.

Before she opened the door, she peered through the slits, listening carefully, but there was no sign of human life anywhere. The night clouds were breaking up; rain drops beat in a sudden flurry across the outbuildings, then ceased falling as abruptly as they had begun.

Julie ducked back inside for her doll and the saddlebag, then hurried up the rain-wet slope to the commissary, where under cover of the building she could look out across the misty parade toward the guardhouse. Nothing moved there.

She entered the building, heading straight for the cellar steps, and went down directly to the shelves where she had found the bright-colored bottles—an eternity of two days ago. Lifting the loose board, she removed the bottles, emptied the saddlebag, and quickly stowed all the packages of Treasury notes into the recess. She then ripped the broken seam along the doll's side, and as she pulled out the cotton stuffing, packed it carefully over the money until none of the green paper showed. In a minute she replaced the bottles, pressing them down into the cotton, and laid the shelf back in place.

With a sigh, she folded the cloth casing of the button-faced doll, thrust it into the saddlebag and went back outside. Dawn was beginning to break in soft gold streaks above the pine-forested east rim. After a final quick look at the guardhouse, she hurried down to the door of the Carlins' kitchen, and was not surprised to find it barred from the inside. With no hesitation, she moved back to the pantry window, and, using the saddlebag as a weapon, forced in one of the glass panes.

A few minutes later she was in the kitchen, gulping water from the indoor pump. As soon as her thirst was satisfied, she began packing Snell's saddlebag with hard biscuits, dried apples, and lumps of brown sugar.

She did not leave by the door but by the window, as she had come, and once outside she wasted no time bridling and laying a saddle blanket over the mule's back, a task which she easily accomplished by offering the half-famished animal a bucket of oats.

By the time the eastern sky was well lighted, she was on her way, urging the mule down through the cottonwoods so that she could not be seen from the guardhouse. At the creek she turned north, for that was the way Captain Westcott had gone.

6

LATE IN THE AFTERNOON OF THE DAY C TROOP LEFT FORT
Wicked, Captain Westcott rendezvoused on the South Fork
with two companies of cavalry from Fort Kinney. The major in
command was operating under orders explicit in only one detail
—under no circumstances was the expedition to divide forces if
the chase led them into the dangerous Porcupine hunting
grounds. Westcott had never met the major before, but after
answering half a dozen astute questions put by that officer, he
was satisfied no time would be wasted or effort spared in pressing hard upon the heels of the fleeing Arapahoes.

At four o'clock the following morning the march north was
underway, the men riding platoon front when the terrain permitted, the three companies spaced a hundred yards apart to
avoid the trailing dust. By holding to a slow steady trot during
the cool of the morning, and by shortening the nooning stop to
half an hour, the column wore away the miles, and camped that
night in the foothills of the Porcupines.

It was during the next morning's march that Peter
Dunreath's alert eyes found a camping site of the Arapahoes,
not more than two days old. Dunreath also discovered something else, and he puzzled over what he saw for several minutes,
squatting on his haunches and carefully studying the markings
in the earth. After he was satisfied with what he read there, he
mounted quickly and rode back to meet Westcott.

"It's a white man's boot, all right," Westcott agreed, when
Dunreath showed him the markings. "But how can you be sure
he was with the party that rode off to the east?"

"Take a look over here." Dunreath moved cautiously, keeping his moccasins clear of the footprints. "The horse he was

ridin' had a bad sand crack. See here where he got down and fooled around for some reason or other, then mounted again. Then off he went, six or seven Arapaho, straight east." He pointed across the sandy rolling plain.

"Why?" Westcott asked aloud, but did not wait for Dunreath to answer. He swung up into his saddle.

"It don't matter why," Dunreath said. "Yankee Snell went east, with a few bucks to keep him company. And from the looks of that sand crack markin', he's needed another horse long before now."

"Mount up!" Westcott ordered impatiently. "We're going to talk to the major."

The major listened patiently to Westcott's report, then rode back along the dismounted column to inspect the tracks for himself. "I suppose we could spare a platoon to follow this up," the major said, "but my objective is the main body. They went into the Porcupines."

"Sir, I request permission to track down this white man." Westcott's jaw tightened as he waited for the reply.

"I said I could spare a platoon, not C Troop. You know my orders, Captain."

"Lieutenant Jackson is fully qualified to command C Troop in my absence, sir."

The major reflected a moment. He was well aware of Westcott's personal involvement in the raid on the wagon train, of his desire for revenge. And if the white man, Snell, had broken away from the main body of Arapahoes, likely enough he would have the stolen payroll in his possession. In this case an officer above the rank of a subaltern might be justified as commander of the pursuing force.

"Very well, Captain. Take your ten best men. And good luck."

"Thank you, sir." Westcott turned toward his mount. "Pete, you're the number one man," he said quickly. "Let's move!"

In less than ten minutes they were on their way east—Westcott, Dunreath, Sergeant Connors, and eight troopers from Connors' platoon. Dunreath rode thirty or forty yards in advance, following the two-day-old trail that would have been indiscernible to an untrained eye. Dunreath read there the full story of Snell's failing mount, the spreading sand crack growing more painful mile by mile, and he was not surprised when the trail swung southward and ended at a ranch. Nor was he surprised to learn there of stolen horses and a fight in which one of the ranchers and two Indians had been killed.

But after the platoon left the ranch, the trail became more difficult to follow. About midafternoon of the second day of the pursuit, along a rugged boulder-strewn ridge, they lost all trace of the hoof markings. Westcott concealed his disappointment and ordered the men to follow him down off the ridge to a circle of green that marked a water hole. The water had a saline flavor, but they filled their empty canteens, and removed the horses' bits and let them drink what they wanted of it.

"Two ways they would not have gone," Westcott said. "East or back north."

"Not Snell," Dunreath agreed. "He's too foxy. But remember he was outnumbered by his Injun friends."

"If you were an Arapaho this far south, not fancying to meet either soldiers or ranchers, where'd you go?"

Dunreath grinned. "I'd go find me some more Arapahoes."

"It's a chancy guess." Westcott pulled the stopper out of his freshly filled canteen and rinsed his mouth with the brackish water. "But we'll head south for that Arapaho village."

Two hours later, Dunreath was riding flank on the west when he saw four horsemen coming up fast from the south along the Bittercreek fork. He whistled and lifted a beckoning hand to Westcott. The captain ordered the platoon to oblique at a fast trot. As the blue-shirted cavalrymen came up on the rise, the four riders from the south saw them, slowed briefly, then veered off toward the Bittercreek and a row of eroded buttes beyond.

"They're actin' kind of shy," Dunreath commented.

Westcott had his field glass on them. "Arapahoes, I think." He passed the glass to Dunreath.

"They sure ain't Shoshoni."

"Front into line!" Westcott shouted. "At a gallop!" As the platoon swept down the sage-grown slope, the four Indians broke into a thicket of aspens, heading for the sandy overflow of the Bittercreek. By the time the cavalrymen reached the stream, the Arapahoes were across the wide shallows, taking cover behind a heap of driftwood and opening fire on their pursuers.

Westcott ordered the platoon to pull back into the thicket.

"They're not going anywhere for a while," he said. "Sergeant, dismount your men, and send the horseholders back a few yards."

Breaking off a chew of tobacco, Dunreath bent and peered through a screen of willow fronds. "It's a split poker pot, Ben. Both sides holdin' high cards. We can't get at them, and they can't get out till we say so, leastwise not till dark."

Westcott lay on his belly, studying the Indians' position. Directly behind them was a flat-faced butte, impossible to climb on horseback. If they attempted to scatter either to right or left, they'd be in easy carbine range. The Arapahoes had to stay where they were until dark—three or four hours yet.

As for the platoon getting at them by charging across the shallow stream, that was patently impossible without suffering severe casualties. Any flanking approach also appeared risky. Reaching for his field glass, Westcott fixed it upon the bluff, studying its height and the formation of the base, eroded by years of spring flood waters.

"Those Arapahoes know something, are guilty of something, or they wouldn't've run like that," he said. "I want at least one of them alive. Pete, you and I will lead our horses far enough back to use the woods for a screen, then we'll head down stream a mile or so to where that butte over there levels out. We can cross unobserved and make our way back so we'll be sitting right over their heads."

Dunreath squinted across the Bittercreek. "From here I'd say they'd still be out of range the way the bluff bellies out midway down."

"We'll have to make our way down to get at them. Look over there to the left." He pointed. "Plenty of foot- and handholds and not too steep. Those fluted crevices will give us cover, once we're down."

Dunreath spat in the sand "*If* we get down, Cap'n. Supposin' they hear us knockin' pebbles about or somethin'? They could pot us easier'n swattin' flies on a honey jar."

"That's where Sergeant Connors gives us a hand. As soon as you see us start down, Sergeant, have your men open fire, successive fire by the numbers. Don't waste ammunition, just keep banging away to cover any noise we may make. Understand?"

"Yes, sir, and I ask permission to go in the capt'n's place, sir, so he may stay with the platoon."

"Permission refused. But if anything goes wrong, you pull out and head for Fort Kinney. That's a direct order."

"Yes, sir."

Dunreath was already untying his horse. "Another thing, Connors," he drawled. "Be sure your carbines are pointed at them Injuns. Don't mistake the cap'n and me for a pair of mountain goats."

In less than an hour, Westcott and Dunreath had made the circuitous crossing downstream and were on the flat-topped butte. From that height they could see some of the troopers quite plainly, spaced through the brush in prone firing positions. They hobbled their horses and made their way on foot to the point of descent. Tightening his cartridge belt and adjusting his carbine in its sling, Westcott led the way down the rough precipice.

Dunreath shook his head dubiously, but followed the captain. They had not gone a dozen yards when Connors started the troopers to firing, and the Indians responded with a few desultory shots. Confident the steady racket would cover any noise they made, Westcott and the scout speeded their descent, disregarding dislodged pebbles and the scraping of their boots on the ledges. They were only a few yards from the sandy creek bank below, when a rock as large as a man's head broke loose beneath one of Westcott's probing boots and rolled with a loud splash into the stream.

As Westcott swung in midair, supported only by his hands gripping a ledge, one of the Arapahoes came charging out from the pile of driftwood. The Indian got off a wild shot at the captain before a bullet from Dunreath's carbine knocked him out of his saddle.

The warrior was floundering about in the milky water, clutching at one shoulder, when Westcott found a new foothold and yelled back to Dunreath. "Keep him covered while I go down and take him alive!"

Westcott crawled around a sharp outthrust of rock, let go, and slid all the way to the moist sand below. He had his revolver ready, crouching, when a volley of carbine fire from Connors' troopers across the stream sent bullets screaming all around him. He saw the dismounted Arapaho fold over in the water and lie where he had fallen, partly submerged, his long black hair washing over his face. The Indian's pony splashed away riderless, whinnying shrilly.

"Damn good shootin'," Dunreath said as he dropped down beside Westcott.

"Too good," Westcott replied dryly. "I wanted him alive. I'm going to try to wing one of the others before they get panicky." He found his hat where it had dropped on the sand, and moved up to a screen of fluted limestone, and peered around it. He fired quickly, dodged back, and a yelp of pain echoed along the bluff. A few seconds later harness metal jingled and horses' hoofs beat with a muffled drumming against the hard packed sand. Connors' response to the Indians' attempted flight was another volley from across the stream, and as Westcott and Dunreath broke out of their cover they saw two Arapahoes making a run for it upstream. The Indians were dead before they traveled fifty yards.

By the time Connors got the platoon in saddles and across the Bittercreek, Westcott had flushed the wounded Indian from behind the driftwood, and Dunreath disarmed him. The Indian had been shot cleanly through the shoulder, but his face showed no sign of pain or emotion. He was the only survivor.

"Ask him if he knows a black-bearded man named Snell," Westcott said impatiently.

Dunreath spoke slowly in Arapaho, but the Indian remained mute. His eyes looked out toward the stream where his brother warrior lay, rocked gently by the lazy current. One of the mounted troopers had turned toward the dead warrior, and was leaning out of his saddle. He reached down, caught at the long black hair and dragged the body ashore.

With a grunt of sudden comprehension, Dunreath said quietly to Westcott: "That one was somebody special, a little chief maybe." He turned back to the wounded warrior. *"Sapa He,* Black Horn?" he asked, keeping his voice casual.

For a minute, not a muscle moved on the captured Arapaho's face. Then he nodded slowly. *"Sapa He,* Black Horn."

Westcott spun around and walked over to the dead warrior and with his carbine muzzle pushed the greasy hair away from the face. In death, with buckskins sodden, and with sand in mouth and eyes, Black Horn looked like any other Indian. *Alive I hated him,* Westcott thought. *Now it doesn't matter. With Snell it will be different because Snell's was the brain behind the raid. Black Horn was only the instrument.*

As he turned back to Dunreath and the captive, he could feel his boots pulling in the washed sand. "Tell him this, Pete. We'll make him a bargain. If he tells us where Snell is, we'll let him go. Give him back his horse and his life."

Dunreath's scraggly eyebrows shot up. "He can lie easy enough."

"We'll chance it. We don't want to be bothered with a prisoner anyhow."

Using elaborate hand signals for emphasis, Dunreath explained Westcott's offer to the Arapaho. The Indian's eyes cut sideways to the captain, suspicious, then he bowed his head and body, and made an affirmative gesture with his right hand.

"Where is the black-bearded one called Yankee?" the scout asked in Arapaho.

The captive spoke, his voice deep, his arms and hands motioning to the south, and he used the English words, *Fort Wicked.*

"You hear that, Ben?" Excitement showed in Dunreath's bright blue eyes. "He says they left Yankee Snell at Fort Wicked. Some kind of trouble. He don't remember much about it, seems they was liquored up."

Westcott's face hardened. "You know as well as I that Brad Carlin would never *willingly* let an Indian at his whiskey." He looked off to the south. The platoon and mounts needed a night's rest, but there would not be much resting now until they were at Fort Wicked.

*   *   *

It was Sergeant Connors who saw her first, along late in the afternoon, off across a tract of prickly pear where butterflies fluttered in swarms like lightly blowing yellow snow. Connors was riding in advance, and when he saw Julie astride the plodding mule, he thought she was a squaw, lost, or separated from her people. He raised in his stirrups, yelling back to Westcott: "Hellfire in the mountains, sir, what's that over there?"

Westcott had been nodding in his saddle. As his head came up, he saw the movement of the mule half a mile away, and his first reaction was to search for other riders. But there were no others, only the mule and the lonely girl in bright-checked calico. He unslung his field glass.

Dunreath pulled up beside Westcott, his eyes squinting at the oncoming rider. "What she look like?"

"It's the girl," Westcott said hoarsely. "The girl from Fort Wicked—Julie!"

"Be damn!"

The scout had to pull aside to avoid Westcott's lunging horse as the captain set spurs to its flanks, and galloped straight away across the plain, disregarding the beds of prickly pear.

By the time Westcott cut into the dusty trail again, the girl had halted the mule. She was sitting with reins clinched in her hands, her bare knees drawn in tightly to the saddle blanket when he thundered down upon her and dismounted.

She was off the mule the instant she recognized him, running toward him, tossing her disarranged hair out of her face, and then rushing into his outspread arms. He kneeled, and she buried her face in his shoulder, shuddering, her body shaken by soundless spasms of relief.

"All right, all right," Westcott said, and caught her shoulders, pushing her back so he could see into her face. Her sun-bleached hair fell over her forehead, and he brushed it away gently. No tears showed in her wide violet eyes.

When he heard the platoon coming up the trail, he turned and signaled Connors to halt the troopers. Dunreath disregarded the order, and walked his mount up behind the captain and the girl. "She tell you what happened, Ben?"

"She won't say," Westcott replied tersely. Julie had pressed her face into his shoulder again, and he spoke softly, his lips against the sunburned shell of her ear. "Tell me about it, girl. Tell me about it and the fear will go away."

He could feel her shivering under his hands, her teeth chattering as she tried to speak his name. Behind them, Dunreath dismounted and took the tie rope of Westcott's horse. "The lassie's sufferin' hy-steerics," the scout said. "Sutler's daughter up at Yellowhorse was like that. Only way her ma could bring her out of them spells was to take her down and thwack her hard across the rump. You want me to do it?"

"No." Westcott gave Dunreath a fierce look, but the girl's dry spasmodic sobs increased in violence.

"You wait too long, she'll suffer real bad," the scout drawled.

"All right, then." Westcott turned her across one knee and brought his hand down sharply in a swift slap across her buttocks, feeling the sting of flesh against flesh through the thin ripped calico. He was suddenly embarrassed, his face reddening, and was utterly unprepared for the reaction, her abrupt squirming away from him, the indignation in her smoky violet eyes, the pained expression of violated modesty. And then the tears came, flooding, and he had to untie his yellow scarf and wipe the moistened dust away from her cheeks.

She told him everything that had happened at Fort Wicked, detail by detail, and he kept sponging away at her tear-streaked face until she had finished. She drew away then, dry-eyed, and looked up at him. "You had no cause to spank me, Captain Westcott," she said in a hurt tone. "And now I'd be obliged to you for a drink of water."

"I'm sorry," he said apologetically, and unstopped his canteen for her. As she tipped the container to drink, a swarm of yellow butterflies drifted lazily across the trail behind her, flickering in the slanting sunlight.

"She's a game little pullet," Dunreath said softly, and added under his breath: "That damned Yankee Snell."

Westcott bent down and picked a shiny gold locket from the dust. "You must've dropped this—"

She finished the sentence for him: "Out of my pocket, when you spanked me." Her lips curved in a sulky smile as she returned his canteen.

Westcott was frowning at the locket. "Where'd you find this?" he demanded harshly, and his thumb pressed the hidden catch so that the case sprang open.

Julie moved closer, standing on tiptoes, holding on to his arm, curious, and then surprised to see the two miniature photographs inside the locket. "Why one of them is you, Captain Westcott. Who's the beautiful lady?"

"Where'd you get it?" he repeated.

"One of the Indians had it around his neck. Brad tore it off in the fight they—"

Westcott snapped the gold case shut, and thrust it inside his

shirt pocket. His eyes held the same dead, burned-out look that
Dunreath had seen in them the day they found Anna Llewellyn's dress on one of the Arapaho squaws.

"I'll thank you to return my gold fancy piece, Captain Westcott." She stood facing him, her voice proud, hands on hips, her
moccasined feet spread apart.

Westcott ignored her, his mouth drawn in a tight line as he
gazed toward the buttes on the south. "Put a lead rope on that
mule, will you, Pete? I'll take the girl up behind my saddle."

"We ought to be makin' camp soon," Dunreath protested
mildly. "The mounts are about beat."

Westcott reached for his reins, his voice raw and edgy: "And
let Snell die of his gunshot wounds before I can find him?"

* * *

But they did not find Yaneka Snell, dead or alive, in the old
guardhouse at Fort Wicked. The door was half-open, the bay
horse was gone, and the only evidence of Snell's former presence were black splotches of dried blood on the prisoners'
bench.

As the ranchers had done, Westcott sent his men out in circling patrols around the basin, but there was no trace of the
bearded man, no recognizable trail that Peter Dunreath could
discover.

The day after Westcott's patrol reached Fort Wicked, a stagecoach from the west drove into the side road and Brad Carlin
dropped off. He was astounded and relieved to find Julie there,
safe and sound in the protection of Captain Westcott's platoon.
Brad still wore a bandage around his head, and he looked pale
and thin, but finding Julie alive was a reviving tonic for him.

That evening while Brad and Westcott sat in the trading
room talking, Julie slipped out and walked down through the
dusky light to Maude's grave. Frogs and insects drowned the
land in summer sounds, yet it seemed peaceful and quiet there
by the fresh mound of brown earth. The girl stood for a long
while, looking first at the grave and then at the stars beginning
to sprinkle across the night sky.

*I just have to talk to somebody, somebody good like you,
Maude, I need to ask somebody about that money he killed to
steal, all the green money I hid away there in the old commissary. All that money, is it like my Ma made me read about in the*

*Holy Bible, is it the root of all evil, which means very, very bad,
like my Ma said? They pierced themselves through with many
sorrows, the Holy Bible said, because money is evil and bad.
Would I be bad, Maude, if I did not tell nobody, not a breathing
soul about the money? Because the captain's sweetheart, Miss
Llewellyn, is dead, and you are dead, Maude, and the Indians
are dead, and maybe that old Snell is dead, too. It's evil and bad,
that money is, Maude, and I won't tell a breathing soul, not
nobody, Maude, where I hid the money so nobody will ever find
it.*

7

A FEW DAYS AFTER WESTCOTT ESTABLISHED COMMUNICA-
tion by telegraph with the Yellowhorse command, he received
the following orders which were to keep him in the vicinity of
Fort Wicked for several weeks:

> C TROOP UNDER TEMPORARY COMMAND LIEUTENANT
> JACKSON EN ROUTE TO FORT WICKED WITH SMALL
> NUMBER OF HOSTILE ARAPAHO CAPTURED BY PUNITIVE
> EXPEDITION INTO PORCUPINE RANGES. THAT EXPEDITION
> NOW WITHDRAWN. UPON ARRIVAL C TROOP YOU WILL
> REASSUME COMMAND AND AS SOON AS PRACTICABLE
> THEREAFTER ARE DIRECTED TO BEGIN ROUNDING UP ALL
> ARAPAHO BANDS IN SOUTHERN TERRITORY
> CONCENTRATING THEM UNDER CLOSE GUARD AT FORT
> WICKED. KEEP THIS COMMAND INFORMED AT ALL TIMES
> OF MOVEMENTS AND REPORT WHEN MISSION COMPLETED.
> THIS ACTION IS OF UTMOST URGENCY.

"It would seem the bigwigs in Washington," Westcott observed when he showed Brad Carlin the message, "have at last
realized the condition of the Arapaho bands and their need for
a reservation."

Brad scratched his head, and read the telegram over again.
"It don't say that here," he replied skeptically. "It just says
bring the poor devils in."

"My guess is the authorities haven't exactly made up their
wishy-washy minds." Westcott smiled, and added: "I've sent off
two mild suggestions to headquarters which may hasten a deci-

sion. I'm recommending you as agent and the abandoned barracks here for agency quarters."

"Ah, now, you know I'd never be an agent and the second part of your recommendation makes too much sense for the Indian bureau to ever follow it up. No, I'll believe it when I see it."

Later in the week, C Troop arrived with the Arapaho captives from the Porcupines, and Westcott began a series of regular patrols to bring in remnants of the scattered bands. This new assignment was to his liking on two counts; first, he believed in what he was doing, and second, it gave him an opportunity to scour the lower territory thoroughly in search of Yaneka Snell.

He persuaded Wolf Moccasin to bring in most of the Sagebrush band, but he did not find a single clue to Yaneka Snell's whereabouts. If any of the Indians had seen or heard of the black-bearded man, none would admit it. One day he realized that he was pushing his men into areas where Arapahoes could not possibly be, only because he hoped to find some rumor or fragment of fact that would lead him to Snell.

That night he telegraphed the Yellowhorse command that his mission was completed: the Arapaho bands were rounded up, and he awaited further orders.

Twenty-four hours later the orders came, ticked out slowly over the field telegraph. After he had read the message, Westcott showed it to Brad Carlin, and said wearily: "You were right all along, Brad. The bigwigs are still shilly-shallying."

" 'Inform Arapahoes they will be admitted to Wind River reservation for winter,' " Carlin read aloud. " 'In view of fact Shoshoni are old enemies of Arapahoes this movement will be strictly voluntary.' " He dropped the message sheet on the floor and uttered a single-worded profane comment.

Westcott sighed. "Most of them will just drift off to the south to eke out the winter. But anyway it leaves me free to ask for leave. I mean to track down Yaneka Snell if it takes the rest of my natural life."

Within a week his request for leave was approved, and he wasted no time in exchanging his cavalry uniform for buckskins. While he was making last-minute purchases of supplies in the trading store, he informed Carlin of his plans. "I've given a lot of thought," he said, "figuring what a man like Yaneka Snell would do with that stolen fortune. He would go where he could spend it, where no one would look twice at a paper Treasury note."

"Supposing he's just plain dead," Brad replied.

"I've thought of that, of course." Westcott paused and frowned, surprised at his own feelings, suddenly aware that if he knew Snell was dead, there would be no purpose in his life. "No, I've searched this basin and all the country round, combed it. There'd be some trace of the horse, that stolen bay, the money."

"Nobody talks about found money." Brad shook his head slowly. "But if he is alive, I got as much cause as you to hunt him down." He hesitated, and went on: "You'll need a partner. I'm going with you, Ben."

A flicker of a smile crossed Westcott's lips. "Much obliged, but no. You can't go, Brad."

"Why not?"

"The girl. Julie."

Brad glanced over his shoulder, and kept his voice low. "What *can* I do with that girl?"

Westcott looked startled. "You're not thinking of—"

"She needs a woman, Ben."

Back in the kitchen a pan rattled, and Julie's voice called out clearly from the curtained area: "Supper's on the table, Brad. And if Captain Westcott is still there, tell him to come share potluck."

Westcott brushed a hand through his shock of red hair, his teeth showing in a broad grin. "*She* needs a woman? She is a woman, Brad. You're going to stay here and raise her up right until I come back. That's an order, you hear me?"

Next day, Westcott rode away to the south. He spent a month in Denver and the larger mining camps of Colorado, another month in the rip-roaring cattle towns of Kansas and Nebraska, and then boarded a stagecoach bound for the Montana gold fields. Everywhere he went he asked about a huge black-bearded man who would likely be a free spender.

At the bar of a cheap saloon in Furnace Creek, Westcott finally found a man who had seen Yaneka Snell. He was a wizened little French-Canadian miner, and he too was looking for Snell.

"For certain, this must be the same man," the miner declared. "Although he told me his name is Smith."

"A big man with a long black greasy beard, staring eyes, hands the size of hams?"

"That is the one."

Westcott could feel his heart thumping with excitement. He bought the miner a drink and invited him over to a table.

"Why are you looking for him?" Westcott asked.

"He very bad man, I tell you. I have this claim down there in Yellowhorse hills, have little shack there, and one day this man come on horse. He was tied in saddle, he so bad hurt and sick with fever. Leg much swelled up and covered with insects. I put him in bunk and try to make him well with balsam sap and some herbs I get from Indians. He stay many days, lying in bunk always. Every day I go up valley to work my claim. One evening I come back, find this big man gone, all my gold dust gone."

That was like Snell, Westcott thought, _repaying the man who saved his life by stealing his gold._

"You say this was in the Yellowhorse hills?"

"Yes. I find good dust there."

Westcott felt a sense of frustration. The Yellowhorse country was almost two hundred miles to the south.

"How long ago was this?"

The French-Canadian shrugged. "Maybe three months."

"And you've found no trace of him?"

"No." The little man studied his empty glass sadly.

Westcott bought him another drink. "Now there are two of us searching," he said. "We can cover twice as much territory."

"Is good, yes. We find him, maybe."

Next morning Westcott took the trail to the west, the French-Canadian turning northward. They had agreed to meet in Virginia City.

The little French-Canadian never reached Virginia City. Long afterward, Westcott learned that the miner had found Snell in a Milk River camptown. Snell had shot him to death and was arrested, but because of discrepancies in witnesses' testimony was spared from hanging and sentenced to serve six months in the camp's jailhouse.

Westcott stayed three days in Virginia City waiting for the miner, and then gave up on the search for Snell, temporarily. His furlough was coming to an end, and he was under orders to report back for duty at Fort Wicked.

8

SPRING CAME LATE TO FORT WICKED AFTER THE WINTER that Captain Westcott was away on leave. Even into May the nights were zero cold, and by day the sun shed little warmth so that leaf buds on the cottonwoods were late, and only willows showed a trace of green.

Early one May morning, Julie was taking a bath in the pantry, and because of the chill in the air she left the door open so that some warmth might enter from the kitchen stove. She lathered herself all over with the sweet-scented soap Brad had ordered from St. Louis especially for her use, scrubbing her neck and ears with elaborate care, for this was a special bath for a special occasion. Captain Westcott was coming in on the noon stage.

She was standing up in the tin tub, pouring warm rinsing water down her back, when she heard Brad stumble in through the rear door. A cold blast swept into the pantry. She shivered and searched for a towel, her eyes tight shut against stinging soap suds.

"Confound it," Brad said, "how many times I told you to keep that pantry door closed when you're naked like that?"

"It's too cold in here when the door's shut."

"You could at least hang a curtain."

She found the towel and wiped soap from her eyes. "Am I so ugly, Brad, you can't stand to look at me?"

He went over to the cookstove and rattled a pan for no particular reason. "It's not that, girl—you'll understand soon enough what I mean—it's because you're too be-damned pleasurable to look at, only I shouldn't tell you that."

"If I'm so pleasurable to look at, why you want me to close the door or put up a curtain so you can't see me?"

"Ah, the hell with it—John-day might come in here."

She didn't answer for a minute. She was busy drying her glowing body, which had rounded out and become more feminine during the winter. "I don't think John-day would scold me, like you are."

Brad picked up a stick of wood and rammed it violently into the stove. "Damn it," he muttered half to himself, "I wish I had a woman around here to talk to you, girl. You're growing up wild as a mustang filly. It's got so every wagon freighter from Cheyenne to Bridger's Fort stops in here to see 'that little gal at Fort Wicked.' I can't watch you every minute, but if I catch one of them skinners laying a hand on you, there's going to be trouble for him and you both."

Julie came into the kitchen wearing a woolen undershirt and a gray petticoat. "What are you talking about, Brad?"

"You heard me. And another thing, you'd ought to wear some kind of covering over your chests—like grown-up women do."

She stopped, looked down at her breasts bulging under the woolen undershirt. "What you mean, Brad?"

"If you don't know what I mean I can't tell you." He broke off, half-grinning. "You're sure never going to need any of them artificial maternal founts they sell in the fancy stores back East."

She looked puzzled, then raised her head haughtily and went on into Maude's old bedroom, where she kept the growing wardrobe with which Brad indulged her.

"Brad," she called out to him. "What do you think the big news is that Captain Westcott wrote about in his letter?"

"Nothing much," he replied, and sat down, frowning at the kitchen table. "Maybe he's going to make patrols down here again."

"Oh, if that was all, he'd have said so," she answered, rustling her crinoline petticoats. " 'I'm bringing you and Julie some big news'—that's what he wrote. Brad, do you think he might be going to propose to me?"

Brad's laughter roared through the kitchen. "Now, that *would* be a piece of news." He chuckled again.

The silence from the bedroom was intense for a minute. "You needn't laugh so big, Mr. Brad Carlin," she said crossly. "In every single letter he always wrote, 'Give my love to Julie.' So there!"

Brad smiled to himself. "All right, but he'll need to have my permission. And you'd better get a hustle on, girl. If it takes you as long as usual to get your fine fixings on, that stagecoach will be here and gone before you're half-dressed."

The stage arrived on schedule that morning, and Brad and Julie were both out front waiting when it pulled to a stop. Captain Westcott was the first passenger down, looking leaner and taller than ever. He was wearing a fresh uniform—tight blue-sky kersey trousers with narrow welts of unfaded mustard yellow at the seams, a forage cap, and a new blue cape with bright yellow lining. He had allowed a mustache to grow, dark red, with the ends curved down so that it gave his face a somber quality.

But when he saw Brad and Julie, a cheerful smile erased the grimness of his expression. Julie flung herself into his arms without a word, and when he bent over to caress her cheek, her lips brushed across his in a trembling kiss.

"You're quite a grown-up young lady," he said, holding her away from him. The wind tugged at her red-ribboned ponytail and twirled her full plaid skirt, revealing red-topped cowhide boots trimmed with brass tips. "New boots, too."

"Tell us what the big news is, Captain Westcott," she begged. Her violet eyes looked expectantly into his, her fingers tightening into his wrists.

He laughed. "All in good time, Julie." He reached out to shake hands with Brad. "Well, you look as if Julie's cooking agreed with you, Brad."

"She's a good little cook, all right. Come on in and have some coffee with the passengers. This is a rest stop, if you've forgotten."

Westcott was surprised at how little the trading room had changed during his absence, even the old carpet-cloth chair was in its regular place by the hearth. There was one difference, however. Instead of Maude standing behind the counter handing out biscuit sandwiches and coffee, a handsome breed boy was there. Westcott recognized him immediately, John-day.

John-day's hair was neatly combed; he was wearing a fancy green velveteen vest and looked clean and prosperous. "Soldier-chief Westcott," he cried warmly, with a flash of white teeth.

"Well, this is a surprise." Westcott turned to Brad. "This boy work for you?"

"Since last fall," Brad replied. "Good boy. But I reckon you know him."

Julie squeezed in closer to the captain. "John-day is my best friend," she explained, looking up at Westcott. "You see, neither of us has a proper mother or father, so we feel a close kinship."

If Westcott had stopped to analyze his feelings then he would have been surprised to recognize a twinge of jealousy. "What about me? I'm a good friend."

"Oh, no," she said, her eyes opening wider. "You're my sweetheart."

"I see." Westcott concealed his smile with a lifted coffee mug. "I suppose there is a difference."

She put her hand in his. "Now, will you tell me the big news?"

In spite of Julie's persistence, Westcott delayed revealing the purpose of his visit to Fort Wicked until after the stagecoach and its noisy passengers had departed. Brad settled the captain into the carpet-cloth chair, with his luggage stacked neatly beside him—a small sole-leather trunk, a traveling bag, his rifle, field glasses, canteen, and lunch box—and then, while John-day cleared the counter, he and Julie brought in chairs from the kitchen.

Julie sat facing Westcott, her elbows on her knees, her chin in her hands. Brad smoked lazily on a stogie.

"This is going to be rather a surprise to you, Brad," Westcott began. "But I'm counting on you to give your consent—"

"Oh, he will," Julie interrupted. "Just you ask him."

Westcott stared at the girl in surprise.

Brad rubbed a moccasin against the floor. "I might as well tell you, Ben," he said with a broadening grin. "Julie here's been thinking the news you're bringing concerns her. She thinks you've come to ask her hand in matrimony."

Westcott attempted to conceal his amazement, but his face reddened perceptibly, and all he could manage was a meaningless stammer. Then he regained his control and bowed to the girl. "The most flattering compliment this old soldier ever received," he declared gallantly. "But let me tell you something, miss, if you want to be a cavalryman's sweetheart I'd advise you to exchange that red ribbon in your hair for a yellow one."

If she was abashed at all, she showed no sign, except to arise and counter the remark Westcott had meant to ease the situation: "All I can say to you, Captain Westcott is, if you want to pay court to me, you'd better be shed of that bristly red mustache!" With a shake of her ponytail she turned and swept out of the trading room, chin held high.

Westcott was nonplused, but Brad was shaking with suppressed laughter, and after a few moments the captain found himself chuckling. He reached for his traveling bag, opened it and withdrew a large packet of papers. "While you're in such a good humor, Brad, I'll spring this on you. I have an authorization here naming you as Indian agent for the new Arapaho reservation."

"No, sirree," Brad replied immediately.

"All it needs is your signature."

Brad's face turned serious. "How'd this all come about, Ben?"

"What turned the trick was arranging to have all the ranchers down here sign petitions asking for a reservation with you as agent. The Indian Bureau pays more attention to citizens than to the military."

"You did all this?"

Westcott smiled. "Let's say I had a hand in it."

"You should've asked me first."

"I did. Last summer. You said no."

"It's still no."

"You can't say no. The reservation headquarters is designated as Arapaho Springs."

"Where's that?"

"Right here. Fort Wicked is now officially Arapaho Springs."

Brad shook his head. "Great day in the morning! Another name for this place. Tipsword's Ranch, Benbow's Base, now Arapaho Springs. Hell, it'll always be Fort Wicked."

Westcott handed him a folded sheet of paper. "Here's your appointment as agent."

"You trapped me, Ben. But I won't sign it."

"Do you want a blue-nosed Easterner sent out here to make a mess of things? That's what'll happen if you refuse the job."

Brad sighed, and thrust the paper inside his shirt. "Give me time to think on it. How long you planning to be here?"

Westcott's eyes twinkled. "Quite a while. My old company, C Troop, and an infantry platoon are en route here now. I'll be in command. We'll repair the barracks here, round up the Arapahoes, and keep order until you decide the Indians are ready to live without soldiers. I'd like to work with you, Brad."

"Ah, hell," Brad said, and pulled the appointment sheet out again. "I'll sign it."

During most of the afternoon, Westcott was busy inspecting the base's buildings, estimating requirements and cost of repairing barracks and storerooms. When he appeared at the kitchen door for supper with Brad, Julie was standing there waiting for him.

"Well," he said teasingly. "I see Miss Julie is wearing a yellow ribbon in her hair. What does this mean?"

She searched his face and gave him a quick triumphant smile. "I reckon it means the same thing as you being shed of your ugly old mustache, Captain Ben Westcott."

In the kitchen, Brad banged the front legs of his chair down and peered out at the captain. "By the holy saints," he shouted, "Ben's red bristle-brush *is* gone, sure enough!"

* * *

The weeks that followed were busy ones for everybody at Fort Wicked. Westcott met with little difficulty in persuading Wolf Moccasin to bring in his Sagebrush band. The winter had been a hard one for them. Few buffalo were left on the hunting ranges, and what little opposition there was from the tribal leaders disappeared as soon as they learned their trader friend, Brad Carlin, was to be their agent.

The widely separated roving bands of stubborn Greasy Faces, however, were harder to find in that vast southern territory, and only a few were willing to exchange their harsh freedom for reservation life.

Westcott was disappointed in the ruling of the authorities to keep the new reservation's settlement on a voluntary basis; he knew that some Indians would come in only to draw annuities, and then be off to roam and hunt again. But he used every

means of entreaty he could contrive, inviting the bands to come
in for ceremonies, and when they were there, he saw that all
were well fed with Longhorn beef.

He soon discovered that John-day was his best emissary. The
obstinate Arapahoes were impressed by the half-breed's fine
clothing, his cartridge belt, shiny holster and revolver, his big-
wheeled spurs attached to high-heeled cowboy boots, and most
of all by his privileged swagger. John-day, Westcott privately
admitted, might not be a model agency Indian, but he served as
a useful galvanizing force in persuading reluctant candidates to
join the new reservation.

When Brad Carlin began the slow process of teaching his
charges how they might become self-supporting, he also found
John-day a worthy advocate. During the winter, John-day had
learned from Brad the operation of the blacksmith shop, and he
now acted as an instructor for those of his tribesmen who
wanted to learn horseshoeing and metal-working. It was John-
day who convinced them that an irrigation ditch was necessary
for growing crops. And when it came to plans for a cattle herd,
the boy was especially enthusiastic, backing Brad up when some
of the tribal elders resisted the agent's suggestion that fences
should be erected before cattle were brought in.

The main drawback to all of Brad's planning was lack of
funds and supplies. He estimated the basin's grass would support ten thousand head of beef cattle, but neither he nor Westcott could persuade government authorities to furnish the tribe
with even a small herd. The Arapahoes would be fed, clothed,
and sheltered, the officials explained, but anything beyond that
was the responsibility of the Indians themselves.

John-day soon grew impatient over delays in obtaining cattle,
and he proposed to Brad that the agent lend him enough money
to buy a small herd. Brad decided the idea was risky. He had
already advanced a considerable amount of personal cash for
badly needed tools and implements, and he was beginning to
suspect that bureaucratic red tape would prevent his recovering
very much of it. He also feared that if he singled out the half-
breed for preferential treatment the others would be jealous,
making for bad feelings. He put the boy off, promising to do
something about the cattle at a later date.

With his native shrewdness, John-day decided to plead with

Julie. He knew that if anybody could persuade Agent Carlin to change his mind, the girl was the one most likely to be successful.

He confronted Julie one morning on the bank of the creek, where she was filling water buckets for washing clothes. "Julie say many times she John-day's best friend," he began.

"Of course," Julie answered him seriously. "We're both orphans and we have to stick together like brother and sister."

"Is so," he said. He explained to her about the beef herd, how badly he wanted it, and wove an elaborate story of how it would bring much happiness to his brother Arapahoes. Then he told her of Brad's refusal to lend him money.

From Brad and Captain Westcott, Julie had absorbed their dogged determination to make the new agency a model, a success where others had failed. She also knew that Brad was worried about money; he had let the trading store run down, devoting most of his time to the agency. "How much money will you need?" she asked suddenly.

"May be five hundred dollar," John-day said gloomily. "Only for small herd. John-day take beef to Laramie next year, and Agent Carlin get money back."

"Five hundred dollars." She could see in her mind the packs of greenbacks hidden away in the cellar of the old commissary, the evil money of Yaneka Snell.

She moved closer to him, putting her cheek against his, like a sister showing affection for a brother. "Meet me here tomorrow morning," she whispered. "And don't say a word to nobody, not a solitary breathing soul."

The boy's teeth flashed in a quick smile. "John-day be here."

All that day Julie worried over the money hidden in the commissary cellar. She had not been near the greenbacks since the day she had hidden them there, avoiding the building as if it sheltered some loathsome pestilence.

That evening after supper she went out into the late summer dusk. The eastern ridge was still lighted by a dying sunset, the familiar pine trees marching down into the basin like green-clad soldiers. She wandered over to the neat, grassed-over mound that was Maude's grave, and silently sought an answer to her perplexity. Was the money still damned with evil, or had time cleansed it of its curse? Would it bring harm to her friend, John-day? Perhaps a little of it would bring no harm, she thought. She could give John-day only a little of it, and test its power for evil.

She went back into the kitchen, rummaging around in the dark pantry until she found the old saddlebag with the spread-winged eagle design, the one that had been Yaneka Snell's. By the light of an oil lamp in the kitchen, she opened the bag and found there the empty doll casing, with its foolish button face, forgotten all these months. She put the doll casing away in her bedroom, then peered through the curtains into the store. Brad was still busy over his agency reports.

When she went outside, she was carrying the saddlebag, an unlighted candle, and a block of matches. She could hear Indian children playing down by the barracks, the barking of dogs, and an occasional shout of a soldier from the infantry camp. To make certain that no one was in the vicinity of the commissary, she circled the building, then entered quickly. Because of its poor condition, Captain Westcott had made no effort to repair this building, and Brad used it only for storing a few plows near the front entrance. She went past the plows, stumbling once of twice over the warped flooring, shuddering when a night bird darted past her and out a window.

From memory, she found her way down the stairs, then cautiously lighted the candle. Spider webs brushed her face when she slipped the board off the recess. The bottles, the cotton stuffing from the doll, and the packets of greenbacks were exactly as she had left them.

Until that moment she had given no thought to the size of the cache, but after a year of helping in the store she had learned something of the value of money, and was astonished now at the heaps of greenbacks stacked there in front of her eyes. Until recently Treasury notes had been curiosities at Ford Wicked, but since the soldiers had come, she had seen quite a number of them. She recognized immediately that most of these were five-dollar notes, with an engraving of a man, a woman, and a dog—all alert, the man supporting an ax, the woman with a babe in arms crouching tremulously in the background.

Even after she counted out a hundred of the five-dollar notes, thrusting them down into the saddlebag, the hoard seemed almost untouched. She was relieved at the thought that she had taken only a little of it as a test of its power of evil. Surely, she thought, a little of the money would not bring harm to her friend, John-day.

A scurrying rodent startled her into action. She replaced the shelf, extinguished the candle, and wasted no time in leaving the old building.

Next morning, as soon as Brad had gone out to begin his daily tour of inspection, Julie slung the saddlebag over her shoulder, and walked down to the shady place by the creek where she had promised to meet John-day.

He was there, concealed in the willows waiting for her. When he saw the saddlebag, his mouth broke into his familiar friendly smile. "Julie bring money for John-day, you bet," he said happily, reaching for the bag.

She tugged it away from him. "Not until you swear an oath."

"Swear oath?" He looked puzzled.

"Put your hand over your heart like this," she said, "and swear you hope to die if you tell a breathing soul where you got this money."

He shook his head, mystified, but did as she ordered. He could scarcely wait to open the bag and count the greenbacks.

"Me go now, tell Brad," he cried.

"You'll tell Brad nothing," she retorted angrily.

"But John-day must tell Brad he go see friends who have cattle. Not tell about money, no." He moved close to her and let her caress his cheek. "Me go now," he repeated impatiently, and patted the leather bag. "Bring fine beef for reservation."

* * *

One afternoon several days later, a thin cloud of dust on the western trail attracted Captain Westcott's attention. He watched the dust from the cavalry camp for a while, then mounted his horse and rode up to Brad Carlin's store, which also now served as the Arapaho agency office.

"Your boy John-day is coming in," he informed Brad. "And he's bringing a small beef herd, just as he said."

"Good God Almighty!" Brad moved over to the window. "You don't suppose the rascal rustled 'em off some rancher's outfit?"

"We'd better find out," Westcott replied. "Get your horse."

They were waiting at the trail turn-off when the half-breed

came whooping down like a cowboy, waving and beating his hat against his leg to turn the cattle in toward the creek. He was leading a spare horse, a lively looking pinto.

"White-face yearlings," Brad muttered. "Better stuff than the government's been sending us to feed the tribe. And a new pony, to boot."

As the bawling cattle made the turn, they scented creek water and picked up speed. John-day swung his horse about, trotting toward Westcott and the agent. "How you like?" he called gaily. "Fine beef, heh?"

"Whose are they?" Brad asked directly.

The boy's innocent eyes opened wide. "They John-day's cattle."

"You have a bill of sale?"

"Bill of sale, what that?"

"A piece of paper showing they belong to you."

He shook his head. "No paper, Agent Carlin. I get from friends on range, way back there on Sweetwater."

Brad glanced at Westcott; the captain was watching the half-breed closely, but he said nothing. "The ranchers back on Sweetwater, they the same you drove cattle for last year?"

"Him same." The boy nodded briskly. "Good friends."

"They sure must be," Brad said dryly. "They wanted money, didn't they?"

"John-day give money."

The agent looked over at the herd, estimating their going price at four hundred dollars or more. "You didn't buy them, or that pinto either, with what I been paying you."

"Give ranchers some money. Give more later when rancher friend come down this way."

"I don't like it," Brad said. "You put them critters behind fences now. We'll talk about it later."

John-day, looking crestfallen, turned his horse and started slowly toward the creek, the roped pinto following, ears up alertly.

Westcott spoke for the first time. "Maybe he charmed those ranchers out of the yearlings."

Brad was shaking his head slowly. "That breed boy sure beats me."

With a smile, Westcott nudged his horse into a walk. "Don't

be too hard on him, Brad. You've got to give the boy credit at least for getting off his rump and doing something. Instead of sitting around crying about the good old days of the buffalo hunts."

* * *

Brad saw no more of John-day that afternoon. He was busy in the store, and also had a bothersome letter that required an answer. A missionary who signed himself Obadiah Metcalfe had written, stating that he would be reporting shortly "to help civilize the heathen Arapahoes." The last thing Brad wanted at the moment was a missionary to add to his other troubles.

As he ate his supper, his moroseness deepened, and he was irritated when Julie mentioned with excitement that John-day had become a sort of hero to the tribe because he had brought in the first beef herd.

"I'd think you'd be proud of him," she said. "Instead you act as if he'd been bad, or something."

"He probably has been bad," Brad replied obstinately. "Wouldn't surprise me to see a posse of ranchers ride in here looking for rustlers."

"Oh, you're worse than an old bear," she retorted. "John-day wouldn't rustle cattle."

The rest of the meal was eaten amid a cool silence, finally interrupted by the jingling of the front bell out in the trading room. "Confound it," Brad protested loudly. "You'd think they'd let a man down his coffee in peace, just once."

"You want me to see who it is?" Julie asked with a slight note of impertinence in her voice.

Brad glared at her. "You stay in here. Likely it's one of Ben Westcott's fresh soldier boys up here to make eyes at you." He swallowed his coffee in one gulp, and went out through the curtains, grumbling.

He had to strain his eyes to recognize John-day, standing in the murky light of the trading room. "Oh, it's you," he said coldly.

"John-day come make talk with Agent Carlin."

"Can't it wait till morning?"

"Make talk now, please, sir."

Brad sighed. He found a match and set flame to the wick of the oil lamp on the counter. His eyes widened when he saw the vermillion paint on John-day's face, the freshly greased hair combed tight with a stiff topknot, the long braid of false hair hanging to his knees, the looped necklace of beads covering his neck and chest. Brad Carlin had seen enough young bucks dressed for courting to know that he was looking at one now.

Strewn on the floor around the boy was a new saddle, a buffalo robe, bright-colored blankets, and the old saddlebag Julie had given him. He opened the bag and spilled out a jumble of beads and moccasins upon the floor. "Pinto pony outside," he said. "All this, and pinto pony. John-day give for Julie."

"For Julie!" Brad's jaw fell slack.

"Julie make fine squaw for John-day."

With an effort, Brad contained his impulse to order the boy angrily from the store. But he remembered the Indian custom; in John-day's eyes the agent was being honored. It would be a gross indignity to order the boy away without palavering.

For fifteen minutes, Brad flattered and cajoled, elaborately avoiding all references to Julie or the sore subject of the beef herd. He examined all the offerings, went outside for an inspection of the pinto pony, and ended the parley by asking John-day to put the animal in the corral.

When he went back inside, Brad settled himself heavily in the old carpet-cloth chair by the fireplace, remembering Maude, as he always did when he used that chair. He wished to God she were alive. Things were moving too fast for him, time was speeding by. He needed help. He had not realized until this night that Julie was grown up, an object of desire, old enough to be married. He knew she was fond of the breed boy, but good God, to be married to him, to become a squaw! His thoughts ran on and on, and he scarcely heard the bell when the door opened. He was relieved to see Westcott standing there, wearing his cavalry cape against the twilight chill.

"You look as if you'd seen a ghost," Westcott said.

"Worse than that," Brad replied morosely.

"Have a brandy with me," the captain suggested. "And your troubles will take wing. Good Lord, what's all this junk here on the floor?"

Brad got up, found Westcott's brandy bottle, and poured him a short glass. "You ever seen a buck come courting, Ben? That junk, as you call it, there, plus a pinto pony, represent the value our friend John-day has placed on Julie."

Westcott set the brandy glass, its contents untouched, upon the counter. He blinked in disbelief. "That breed boy wants Julie?"

"You heard me."

"You sent him packing, of course."

"I handled it, no hard feelings."

Westcott took a quick swallow of his drink. "Does Julie know?"

"Nah, I don't know how to put it to her. Hell fire, that wild young-un might take him up on it."

"That's her privilege," Westcott said soberly. "How old is she, Brad?"

"Hell, I don't know."

Feeling the warmth of the closed room and the brandy, Westcott removed his cape; he unslung his revolver belt and placed it on the counter beside the cape. "Call her out here, Brad."

A moment after Brad called her name, Julie thrust her head through the curtains, her nose crinkling as she smiled at Westcott, the sly secretive smile he had learned to expect from her.

Brad chided her: "You were listening, girl, I can tell."

She came and leaned her elbows on the counter, her violet eyes no more than a foot from Westcott's. "I've got good ears, Brad."

"Brazen as a hussy," Brad muttered.

"How old are you, Julie?" Westcott asked seriously.

She turned her head sidewise. "Well, now, I don't rightly know. When I came here I was fifteen going on sixteen, so now I must be sixteen going on seventeen."

"When's your birthday?"

"I don't know."

"Didn't your ma tell you, or your pa?"

"Ma must've told me, but I reckon I was too young to remember."

Brad slapped his hand on the counter. "Let's get down to cases. You heard John-day and me talking when he was here, while ago?"

She raised her eyebrows coyly. "Most every word."

"Well?"

"Well what, Brad?"

"You don't want to marry up with that moonshiny half-breed, do you?"

She rested her chin on one finger tip, looking at Westcott's worried face as she replied: "Well, now I might." She paused and glanced back to Brad. "John-day's a good boy, Brad, but I can't marry him, because, you see, I'm going to marry Captain Westcott."

9

JULIE WAS ALREADY AWAKE WHEN THE MORNING GUN
boomed, rattling the shutters above her head. When she opened
the window, a warm earthy fragrance on the early breeze told
her that spring had really come for certain after another long
winter at Fort Wicked. Soon she would be seventeen going on
eighteen, and Captain Westcott had not yet asked her to marry
him.

She rolled out of bed and reached for a rose-tinted wrapper,
beribboned and fluffy and filmy—a Christmas present from
Brad—and went out into the kitchen. When she opened the
door to let in the spring aromas, she saw the flag fluttering to
the top of its pole down in the cavalry camp, and then the
peaceful morning was shattered by a shrill reveille of infantry
fifes and drums.

As if to celebrate the end of winter, the drums rolled louder
and louder, then died away while three or four bugles played a
merry little air—all finally drowned out by the howling and
barking of the Arapahoes' dogs farther up the creek and the
sounds of roll call echoing through the greening cottonwoods.
She turned away dreamily and went back into her room.

Stretching languidly across the bed, she propped her feet on
the window sill, and pondered the problem of Captain Ben
Westcott. It wasn't that she had not given him plenty of oppor-
tunities during the winter to tie a true lovers' knot. At the
Saturday night dances for the soldiers she had been the belle of
the ball. None of the ranchers' wives or daughters had half the
offers for dances as she, yet she had given most of them to that
redheaded scrimshanker of a captain, whose blue eyes told her
he loved her but who kept a tight bridle on his tongue. He had

taught her to dance the galop, the guards waltz, and the Boston dip, yet even while he held her in his arms he was seemingly oblivious to her charms, and nothing she could say or do even encouraged him to offer her more than a fatherly kiss.

Yet she remembered one cold winter evening—the first real blizzard of the season—when Westcott had burst into the store full of excitement. He was wearing a long buffalo coat, muskrat cap, and winter gauntlets—the fur from his head down sprinkled with snow and hung with icicles. On a routine patrol he had come across an itinerant photographer whose wagon was bogged down in a drift, and Westcott brought him in with all his equipment, more with the object of having him photograph Julie than saving the poor fellow's life.

She rolled over on her stomach, recalling how Westcott had insisted she dress as a little girl for her portrait, with her hair fixed in that silly ponytail she had abandoned months ago, and how she had quarreled with him because she wanted to wear her low-necked dance frock that revealed her fine snowy shoulders. In the end she struck a bargain with him; she would dress as he wanted provided he sat with her, and she had the photograph now, over there on her dressing table. Brad said Ben Westcott in that picture bore the expression of a cornered wolf, but she thought the two of them looked like true lovers.

Out in the kitchen she heard someone moving around, and she guessed it was the rancher from Sweetwater, the one who had come down to collect a hundred dollars he claimed Johnday still owed him for the cattle and that pinto pony. Brad had bedded the rancher in the pantry last night, after informing the man that so far as he knew John-day had not a penny to his name, but that the pony and some of the cattle could be reclaimed for full value due.

Late yesterday she had a perfectly furious quarrel with Johnday, who insisted that she must supply him the necessary hundred dollars. If he lost any of his cattle, he wailed, he would lose his high standing in the tribe, and as for the pinto, that pony was the same as his brother. She pointed out that but for the kindness in Brad's heart the pinto was legally hers, since he had made a marriage offer of it. They had quarreled over that, bitterly. To be rid of his lamentations, she finally made a vague promise to help him, and after dark she went unwillingly to the dingy, cobwebbed cellar of the old commissary building and took twenty more five-dollar notes from Yaneka Snell's evil hoard.

She had the greenbacks now, rolled into the toe of one of her moccasins, and thinking of the money reminded her it was time to be up and dressed and at work preparing breakfast for Brad and the rancher from Sweetwater.

During the meal she smiled secretly to herself when she heard Brad inform the rancher that as soon as breakfast was finished they would find John-day and ride down to the fenced pasture, and there settle the claim. She knew they would not find John-day until she had seen him, because the half-breed would be hiding down in the willows by the creek waiting for her.

As soon as the men went out to the corral, she slipped through the kitchen door and walked straight down to the willows. John-day was there, with his saddled pinto concealed back in the green brush. Because he looked so completely unworried, she was immediately provoked into teasing him.

"Julie have money?" he asked expectantly.

"No money," she replied haughtily. "You should not have traded for more than the five hundred dollars I gave you last time."

"But John-day need offerings for Julie," he protested. "Five hundred dollar not enough for offerings for Julie, and cattle herd also."

His anguished face, the outright dejection in his soul and body softened her, and she thrust the roll of greenbacks into his hand. "Swear the oath," she whispered, and waited until he had done so before releasing her fingers. "And hope to die!" she repeated, when he rubbed his cheek against hers in gratitude. He turned abruptly and picked up the old eagle-marked saddlebag that had once been Yaneka Snell's, pushing the greenbacks down inside it.

"They're up at the corral," she told him. "Brad and that rancher."

"Hokay," he said, grinning at her, and jumped astride the pinto.

He rode in a fast trot toward the corral, breaking into a

gallop as he saw Brad and the rancher riding away toward the Arapaho quarters.

"Ho, Agent Carlin!" he called, and swung up beside them, dancing his pony.

"Looked all over for you last night," Brad said gruffly. "Where you been?"

"No place," the boy said innocently.

"You got to give that pinto back to this man. Some of the cattle, too."

John-day shook his head slyly. "Me promise to pay hundred dollar."

"You haven't got a hundred dollars," Brad declared firmly.

"Have so." He unstrapped the saddlebag and brought the greenbacks up in a wad, kneeing the pinto expertly in beside the rancher as he held his clenched hand outward.

The rancher glanced at Brad, and took the money.

"Let me see that stuff," Brad cried. "Greenbacks, ain't it?"

With a shrug the rancher handed over the notes. Brad held one up to the sun, snapping it flat. "Looks legal to me," he said. "Same as soldiers' pay. Where in hell did you get this paper money, John-day?"

"Cattle and pony all for me now?" the boy asked, peering anxiously into the rancher's face.

"Does it add up to a hundred?" the rancher asked Brad.

"It's a hundred all right."

"You keep it, Brad," the rancher said. "I can't use that paper up on the Sweetwater. I'll take it in trade."

"John-day go now?" the boy spoke up shyly.

"Wait a minute." Brad's voice was harsh. "You didn't tell me where you found this green stuff."

"No can say." The boy's eyes grew round and frightened.

"The hell you can't. Who gave it to you?"

John-day let his pony dance away a few yards. "Swore oath to die. No can say."

Brad shot a quick glance at the rancher. "What did he pay you with, mister, when he bought that herd last fall?"

The rancher looked worried. "Greenbacks. I had to take them clear in to Denver and took a discount, too."

"Six hundred in greenbacks. Jee-sul!" Brad whirled in his saddle. "Ride that damned pinto up to my store, boy. I'm going to get to the bottom of this if I have to skin your hide off. Move!"

As they crossed by the rear of the trading post, Brad cut in toward the kitchen door. "Julie!" he called. The anger and urgency in his voice brought her to the door in a few seconds. "Hurry down there to the cavalry camp and bring Captain Westcott up here. Right now!"

After the horses were tied to the rack in front of the store, Brad calmed his feelings, quietly ordering the boy to follow him and the rancher inside. While he waited for Westcott, he set about collecting the goods which the rancher wanted in exchange for the greenbacks. John-day stood by the counter, a woebegone expression upon his olive-skinned face.

By the time Westcott arrived, the counter was piled high with sacks of meal and flour, boxes of dried fruit, and bags of beans and coffee. The captain came in alone, wearing his field hat and an old sack coat.

"Where's Julie?" Brad asked.

"She went around back," Westcott replied. "She seemed to be scared."

"Scared?" Brad frowned. "Scared of what?"

"You tell me."

"Never mind," Brad said. "I think I've got wind of something may help us find out where the bucks are getting their whiskey."

The rancher glanced at Westcott and drawled: "You folks having trouble with whiskey getting to your Indians? Same thing's happening up at Wind River."

"We can handle it so far," Westcott declared cautiously.

"Ah, hell," Brad said. "We might as well admit it's getting worse every day."

The captain's face reddened slightly, as he turned back to Brad. "You said you'd found out something?"

"This." Brad dug the roll of greenbacks out of his pocket and slapped it down on the counter. "John-day paid out on his herd and the pinto with this stuff. And made the first payment with the same kind of money."

Westcott's glance shifted from the money to the half-breed boy, who was standing far down the counter with panic in his eyes. "Where'd he get it?"

"He won't say."

"Where'd you get the greenbacks, John-day?"

The boy shuffled his feet, his big-wheeled spur digging into the counter facing. "Me swore oath to die. No can say."

"That's what he told me." The agent's voice was querulous. "We could thrash it out of him, maybe, or give him a taste of your guardhouse irons until he finds his tongue."

Westcott frowned at Brad, shaking his head, and spoke so softly his voice was barely audible: "You forget he's part Indian." He walked slowly down the counter, towering over the boy. His voice changed, the words coming out like a whip: "What does John-day know of whiskey traded to his Arapaho brothers?"

The boy almost cringed; it was as if he had been lashed unjustly with a real whip. "No, no, Soldier-chief Westcott. John-day no trade whiskey."

"You'll swear an oath to that, too?"

"I swear. Hope to die."

"If I find you've lied, boy, you'll wish you were dead."

"John-day always talk straight."

Westcott turned his back on him. "Get out of here," he said sternly, and waited until John-day had gone out the front door, waited until the bell stopped jangling.

Brad was frowning at the captain, his forehead furrowed in perplexity. "You just going to let him run out like that?"

"I'll see that he's closely watched," Westcott replied. "But what we need to find out is what he's been up to, last autumn and since. Where's Julie?"

"She's got nothing to do with this," Brad protested.

"No, but maybe she can tell us what John-day's been thinking, what he's been doing. They're as thick as thieves, you know that."

Brad jerked his thumb toward the kitchen. "You talk to her, Ben. I wouldn't know what to say."

Westcott circled the counter and went back into the kitchen, but Julie was not there. He called her name once or twice, then looked out the back door. She was far down the path, running toward the creek. He guessed that she had been listening to what had been happening in the store. Wondering what she was afraid of, he stepped out the door and followed the path unhurriedly as if he were strolling back to the cavalry camp.

When he approached the creek, he heard splashing above the normal sound of running water, and as he stepped up on a small knoll bedded with Indian paint brush, he saw her out in the middle of the stream. Her skirt was hitched up almost to her thighs, and he knew she had seen him, though she gave no sign, turning her back and pretending to be engrossed with the crests of saffron foam spinning by.

Westcott sat down, waiting patiently, knowing how icily cold the water was, wondering as time passed how she could bear the cold as long as she did, and then as he had known she would, she turned abruptly and came splashing toward him, pretending surprise to see him sitting there watching her.

Her legs were goose-fleshed from the shock of cold water, her lips trembling slightly as she waded ashore. She did not bother to lower the skirt, looped and tied behind her slim buttocks, moving with all the artless innocence of one of the Arapaho women who sometimes swam naked in the summer. To Westcott she was like some bright young nymph rising from the waves in a glory of unashamed womanhood. Within him he felt a surge of longing for her that he had not known before, and he wondered how he could ever have thought of her as a willful child rather than a woman to be desired for her womanness.

She forced a low whistle between her teeth, clenched tight so they would not chatter, and came striding bare-legged across the sand to the knoll. He rose and offered her his yellow scarf, and said gravely: "You'd better dry off a bit. The wind will freeze you."

With that secretive smile which had become so familiar to him, she sat down and began rubbing beads of moisture from her knees and upper legs, and he felt his cheeks burning as he watched her dabbing the cloth with the shamelessness of a child and then she said: "My skirt is all knotted back there, Ben Westcott. You might at least offer to untie it."

He kneeled close behind her, staring into the sheen of her pinned-up auburn hair, noticing the faint freckles on the back of her lovely neck, his fingers awkward in the folds of cloth. When the knot loosened, she switched the skirt under her and flipped the hem down over her knees, leaning back against him and gazing up at the spring sky. "I love the clouds like that, don't you, Ben Westcott? Fluffy like clean old sheep."

He put his hands over her shoulders, marveling at the softness of them, and she leaned farther back so that her head was in his lap, her violet eyes smiling up at him. Again he felt the surge of desire, and she must have read it in his eyes. Her lips parted, and the words came out in a whisper: "Put your mouth on mine."

As he kissed her he felt her lips open full, at first in wonderment, and then with a warm unsophisticated passion that needed no tutoring to communicate its meaning. She turned herself in his arms, her breasts straining against him, and she pulled his hand down against her thigh so that he felt the coolness of flesh beneath the cloth.

When at last they broke apart, both sighed in unison, and then she laughed. "You're a wonder," Westcott said softly. "A wonder." He looked around him, suddenly aware of their exposed position. Willows screened them from the soldier camps, but the trading post was in full view up the slope, and seeing it reminded him of why he had followed Julie to the creek.

She rested her head against his shoulder, humming one of the waltz tunes she had learned the past winter. The wind ruffled her hair, mingling the woman scent of her with the blossomy odor of the buffalo currant bushes, bright with yellow flowers downstream. Her lips brushed his ear. "What *are* you thinking about, Ben Westcott?"

"Mostly moonshine and jimcracks," he said. He wanted to tell her he adored her. He dreaded breaking the spell, the splendor of this captured moment in which time was stopped by springtime and love.

"What's John-day been up to?" he said gravely.

She wrinkled her nose at him, and he could see that she was annoyed. Was it because he had broken the magic, or because she did not want to talk about the half-breed?

"He had quite an amount of greenbacks," Westcott went on. "Too much for an Indian to have by chance. Brad suspects he's mixed up with whiskey-running. Somebody's been supplying the Arapahoes with whiskey, you must know that."

She stood up, turning her back on him. "Look," Westcott

continued, "Brad's in trouble. He'll be in more trouble if we don't stop the whiskey runners. Surely Brad means more—"

With a stamp of her bare foot, she swung around, facing him defiantly. "You've no right to accuse John-day! He's done no wrong. He's good, he's not bad."

"All right, then. How did he come by the greenbacks?"

"That's John-day's secret," she cried, and then dropped her voice. "If I'll swear to you he did not get the money from whiskey or any other bad thing, will you believe me?"

"Of course I'll believe you, Julie." As he spoke he could see relief come into her eyes.

"Then I'll swear."

He moved toward her, catching her in his arms, her tears warm against his cheek as she kissed him again, but this time more like a frightened child than a woman.

* * *

Brad and Julie heard the news first from Sergeant Mike Connors, who came hurrying into the store the next morning, wanting several twists of tobacco. "We may be gone a long spell," Connors said, "and I don't want to run out of 'backy. I like my pipe of evenin's."

Brad's question was casual: "Where you troopers patrolling this time?"

"Ain't you heard?" the sergeant asked in surprise. "Troop's got orders to march north. Old Prayerbook Comstock is chasin' Cheyenne again, and we got to help pull him out of the fire. Yes, sir, we're hell-bent for a rousin' ride!"

Julie, who had been sweeping the hearth, dropped her broom and went around the counter, stopping beside Brad. Her face was dead white.

"First I'd heard." Brad pushed the tobacco across the counter.

"I reckon the capt'n's been so busy since he got orders this mornin' he's had no time to pass the word to you." Connors shook his head. "Well, I'd best be hoppin' m'self. See to it the horses' bits fit proper, and all that, you know." He grinned, waved his hand, and was gone.

Julie's fingers were gripping into Brad's arm. "All right, girl," he said calmly, "we'll go down and see him. This couldn't've happened at a worse time, but that's soldiering, as Ben Westcott will tell you himself."

They found Westcott in his sparsely furnished quarters, a boarded-up room in one end of a storage building near the cavalry camp. He was packing his gear, and apologized for not having informed Brad earlier of C Troop's orders. "I was just on the point of saddling my horse to ride up there. Now you've saved me the trouble. We're moving out in two hours, forced march to join Colonel Comstock." He spoke rapidly, continuing his packing, then turned and surveyed the room. Nothing was left but a bare Army cot, two chairs, a square pine table covered with a cavalry blanket, a cigar box half-full of smoking tobacco, another one half-filled with white beans and a pack of cards.

He pulled the blanket off the table and began rolling it.

"The Army couldn't've picked a worse time for this," Brad said. "Whiskey-running, and now a missionary coming in to thicken the air."

"You'll still have the infantry platoon to keep things tight. Chances are that whiskey trouble is the work of one man. Find him and you break it up."

"And what do I do with that missionary, Obadiah what's-his-name—Metcalfe?"

Westcott smiled. "If he's a good man he'll make your work easier."

Julie moved in front of Brad. "When will you be back?" Her voice was thin, almost tearful.

Westcott stared hard at her. "As soon as the Good Lord and the Yellowhorse command will permit." He turned, placing his hands on her shoulders. "I promise you I'll be back, Julie."

"I want to go with you."

He shook his head. "You asked me that one time before. Not so long ago, either, but you were a little girl then." He brushed a tear from below one of her eyes, then reached into his pocket, withdrawing the gold locket he had taken from her the day he met her near the Bittercreek, when she was fleeing from Yaneka Snell. "Remember this?"

She nodded, her voice choking.

"I don't have a ring," he said softly. "This locket will have to do for now." He turned to Brad. "Is it all right with you, Brad?"

"What are you driving at?" Brad demanded suspiciously.

Westcott flushed, running a hand through his red hair. "You're not such a blockhead you don't know what it means when a man offers a woman a ring."

"A woman? A ring?"

"Confound it, Brad Carlin, I'm asking for your daughter's hand." He jammed his field hat down over his rumpled hair. "And I don't have much time to wait for an answer."

"Hell fire, you dumb fool, ask her!" Brad turned his back and walked out into the morning sunlight, into the noise of the assembling cavalry troop. He felt as if he were a million years old.

10

DURING THE WINTER WEEKS THAT YANEKA SNELL SPENT AS an enforced guest in the log jail of a law-abiding mining community on Milk River, he was visited frequently by a wandering missionary named Obadiah Metcalfe. At first, Snell was churlish to his visitor, insulting him and attempting to shock him by using the vilest language at his command. But Metcalfe gave no evidence of being either shocked or outraged.

When the missionary asked the prisoner to pray for forgiveness for slaying a fellow man, Snell replied that he did not need to pray because he was innocent of wrongdoing. He had defended his own life, he declared, and was unjustly imprisoned.

"Then let us pray against man's injustices," Metcalfe cried. "How you must suffer, Mr. Snell, from this grievous wrong!"

"It ain't so bad," Snell said, patting his bulging belly. "They feed me plenty, and being's it's wintertime, I'd be holed up anyway in a cabin somewheres no bigger'n this. Only thing different, I'd have me a plump squaw. That's all I miss."

Instead of expressing disapproval at Snell's remarks, Metcalfe appeared to be fascinated. His beady eyes gleamed under his bushy eyebrows, and he asked Snell if he had known many squaws.

Snell was not long in detecting rascality beneath the thin veneer of righteousness worn by Obadiah Metcalfe. He also discovered the missionary's weakness for liquor, and they spent many a winter afternoon drinking together—good whiskey procured by Metcalfe with some of Snell's secreted gold pieces.

Metcalfe sober was a drab little man with a corded neck, gray skin, and pointed prying nose. But under the influence of liquor his eyes shone, his arms gestured grandly, and words flowed from him in a river of disorganized eloquence.

He told Snell of his dream—of how he would bring his message to the heathen tribes in their reservation camps and create a new civilization. When Snell asked him what his message was, Metcalfe replied: "Glory. Grace and glory. A heavenly kingdom on earth." His eyes blazed with an inner fire of madness. "Saints and the light. Glory. Power and glory. Praise ye the Lord!"

Snell passed him the bottle.

When spring came, Obadiah Metcalfe went south, armed with papers from his Baltimore missionary society authorizing him to bring the word of truth to the Oglala Sioux.

A few days later Snell was freed from jail, and ordered to leave the mining camp. He trimmed his black beard, purchased a pack mule, several gallons of alcohol and some molasses for coloring, and also turned south. While Obadiah Metcalfe preached his message of glory to the Oglalas, Snell established a base a few miles from the reservation and sold these same Indians a mixture of alcohol and molasses liberally cut with creek water. Before the summer ended, he narrowly escaped arrest by the military authorities, and quickly departed for the booming town of Goldfield.

There he found gambling tables and women in plenty, and by autumn much of his gold was gone. He joined on with a gang of buffalo hunters, and hunted all the way north into Canada. Snell brought his hides back into Goldfield, and after collecting his money from the dealer, he prepared to settle down for another season of gambling and women.

One evening as he was entering the El Dorado bar, he saw a familiar figure sitting forlornly on the wooden steps, a drab man in a long-tailed black coat. "Damn me!" Snell cried, slapping the missionary on the back. "If it ain't Obadiah Metcalfe!"

Metcalfe raised his thin elongated nose. "It's indeed a pleasure to see you again, Mr. Snell."

"I thought you was preachin' to the Oglalas."

Metcalfe shook his head. "I fear, sir, they failed to comprehend my message."

Snell grinned. "Come on in, have a drink." He added maliciously: "To glory hallelujah."

Over his drink at the El Dorado bar, Metcalfe poured out his
grievances at the Oglalas, the Indian agents, and Army officers.
Then he told Snell of his present difficulties. His missionary
society had procured a new assignment for him at Arapaho
Springs, he said, but the stubborn agent there refused to accept
him. "I've always longed to bring light to the heathen
Arapahoes, but the agent has shut his hard heart against me."
Metcalfe belched and looked sadly into his empty glass. "A
man named Carlin," he said bitterly.

"Carlin?" Snell's large eyes bulged suddenly, and one of his
huge hands came down hard on Metcalfe's shoulder. "Brad
Carlin?"

"That's him, a son of Satan."

"Arapaho Springs, you said. Where's that?"

Metcalfe pulled free from the pressing hand. "I believe the
place is sometimes called Fort Wicked. Fittingly so."

Snell ordered a fresh bottle and as he drank he let his
thoughts run. So Carlin was still alive, and an agent for the
Arapahoes at Fort Wicked. He had a grudge to settle with that
bastard. Maybe he could fix Carlin and that snippet of a girl
who ran off with his precious saddlebag full of greenbacks. Especially her. He'd fix her in more ways than one if he ever got
his hands on her again. It wouldn't be hard to stir up plenty of
trouble for Carlin. Run whiskey in there. Have to be careful,
though. If that red-haired Westcott was anywhere around,
plenty careful. The Greasy Faces wouldn't likely all be on the
reservation, they were not reservation Indians. They could be
used. And the boy John-day. Ought to see that boy again before
he grew up and forgot who his father was. He could use John-
day. And Obadiah Metcalfe. That spike-nosed missionary was
the key to trouble for Brad Carlin. Must be a way to snake that
glory glory buzzard onto the reservation.

"I know this agent, the man Carlin," Snell said quietly. "He's
a bad one. Wants to keep the Indians heathen. I'd like to help
you drive him out."

Metcalfe's eyes were narrow points of light, "Praise ye the
Lord!" he cried drunkenly.

"Tell you what you do, Obadiah," Snell continued. "You
write a letter back to that mission outfit of yours and ask 'em to
send somebody to see the guv'ment people at Washington. Lay

it on strong. Tell 'em Carlin is keeping the Lord's word from the Arapahoes."

Snell was barely literate, but the next morning after Metcalfe was fully sobered, the two of them composed a letter to the Baltimore missionary society. It was Snell's opinion that if anything happened as a result of the letter, it would not happen soon. He gave Metcalfe enough money to keep him from starving for a few weeks, and ordered him to sit tight in Goldfield and await a reply from his missionary headquarters. In the meantime, Snell would go down to the French miner's shack in the Yellowhorse hills and learn what he could from his old comrades, the Greasy Faces.

After loading two pack mules with strong red whiskey, he started on his way.

Within a short time, Snell was making overtures to occasional small bands of Arapahoes who were hunting in the Yellowhorse hills. From them he received the unwelcome news that Captain Westcott was stationed at Fort Wicked. He also learned of the agency's voluntary policy, of how all Arapahoes were welcome to come in but none was forced to remain. Some of the Greasy Faces had visited the reservation for handouts and tribal ceremonies, but few had stayed.

Snell shared his liquor generously with these Indians and assured them that more would be forthcoming if they would pass the word to the reservation bucks that whiskey was available north of the basin. He would trade for blankets, horses, almost anything, and he would not haggle over values set by the owners. On a certain night he would be here, on another night, there. He would be glad to see all his old friends, the Sagebrush men as well as the Greasy Faces.

And so it was that Yaneka Snell gradually established his whiskey line into Fort Wicked, at the same time prudently keeping far afield from Captain Westcott's cavalry patrols. When his stock of liquor was exhausted, he packed his mules with blankets and robes taken in trade, and with a string of second-rate horses obtained in the same way, returned to Goldfield for a fresh supply of liquid merchandise. He also was anxious to learn what Obadiah Metcalfe might have heard from his home mission.

With some impatience, Metcalfe was awaiting Snell's promised return to Goldfield. Metcalfe had already received two or three communications from his society, as well as an impressive document from government officials authorizing him to proceed immediately to Arapaho Springs and "inaugurate a program of enlightening and improving the moral and religious station of the Arapaho tribe." The agent at Arapaho Springs, Metcalfe was assured, had been instructed to cooperate fully.

"Should you not have come back in another week," Metcalfe told Snell, after he had read him the letters, "I would have felt duty bound to go on without your good company."

Snell grinned. "Why, you don't even have a horse, Obadiah. I'll buy you a good saddle mount and we'll travel together as far as my cabin. Lots of things to tell you about that agent Carlin."

On the ride down to the cabin, Snell cunningly worked on the missionary's prejudices and cupidities, first inventing lies about Brad Carlin's wickedness, then promising to supply money to Metcalfe so that he might bring to fruition his vague dreams of civilizing the tribes. One thing he made clear to the missionary: on no account was he to mention the name of Yaneka Snell. "Carlin hates me because I befriend the Indians," Snell explained piously. "If he knew I was helpin' you he'd stop at nothin' to be rid of you, Obadiah."

After resting for a day at the cabin, Snell rode with the missionary to the north rim of the basin. He picked his time so they would arrive there after dark. They camped under Twin Buttes by the creek, and before dawn Snell rolled the missionary out of his blankets. "This is as far as I go, Obadiah. You just follow the trail along the creek and you'll be to Fort Wicked 'fore dark."

Snell gazed cautiously out over the lighting basin. This was the closest he had been to Fort Wicked since the day of his fight with the Carlins, and he felt a twinge of fear.

"I sure do appreciate your many kindnesses, Mr. Snell," Metcalfe said. "The Lord will reward you."

"Don't speak my name down there, Obadiah," Snell said warningly.

"No, sir," the missionary replied.

The bearded man swung into his saddle. "One more thing," he said. "There's a boy down there. Name of John-day. Tell him his father will meet him here. Tell him to come to the Twin

Buttes, where the creek runs." Snell repeated the instructions. "Tell him to come in three days. His father orders it, tell him."

Metcalfe nodded, and raised his hand, and the horsemen started away in opposite directions, the one back toward the north, the other south toward Fort Wicked.

* * *

Three nights later Yaneka Snell was waiting under the Twin Buttes, back in a cedar thicket a hundred yards or so from the creek. After sundown the air bore an unseasonal bite of frost that penetrated his buckskins. He built a fire of dry wood between two rocks, forming a bed of smokeless coals, and he sat hunched before it, listening for sounds of movement on the trail.

Near midnight he almost gave up, deciding the boy was not coming, and was about to stretch out for a nap when he heard a horse approaching slowly from the direction of Fort Wicked. He moved quickly away from the fire and worked his way down through the cedar clumps until he could see the trail under the starlight. A horseman had slowed to a walk, and was looking first to the right and then to the left, as if expecting to see something or someone.

When the rider was less than fifty feet away, Snell cupped his hands over his mouth and made an odd birdlike call. The rider halted. Snell repeated the sound, and it came back almost as an echo.

Snell stepped out into the trail, his revolver ready. "John-day?"

"Yes, is John-day." The voice was high-pitched, but with an adult undertone strange to Snell's ears.

"Bring your pony back up in the thicket." Snell led the way over the rocks to the fire. He dropped a few sticks on the coals, and as they flamed up he turned to look at the boy. John-day was wearing a bright blue shirt trimmed with scarlet fringe. Curiosity and fear were mixed in the outright stare he gave the bearded man.

"You're late, boy," Snell said brusquely.

John-day said nothing.

"Get your blanket down. We'll lie here and talk. As I said, it's late."

The half-breed unfastened his blanket roll and saddlebag and dropped them on a level place near the fire.

Snell kneeled and warmed his hands over the small blaze. "Why did you come?" he asked suddenly.

"Missionary say father command me come. John-day come."

"Your ma taught you that, didn't she?"

With a shrug, the boy bent and unrolled his blanket, pushing the saddlebag forward for a pillow.

"She was a good squaw, your ma, always did what I said, no back talk. Whatever Yankee Snell said was law, and she taught you that." Snell stretched his powerful arms, yawning. "You're a good boy, John-day."

When the firelight brightened, Snell's eyes shifted to the saddlebag. Something in the leatherwork was familiar, the crude design of a wing-spread eagle. He'd once had a bag made up like that by a blacksmith at Laramie, cost him plenty. By God, that was the bag he'd used to carry the payroll greenbacks! He stooped and ran his fingers over the eagle design and the fastenings. "Where'd you get this saddlebag, boy?".

John-day turned under his blanket, his eyes widening with fear when he saw the cruelty in the bearded man's face. "Julie give me," he answered simply.

"Julie?"

"She girl. Live with Agent Carlin."

Snell felt the quick throb of his heart under his buckskin shirt, but he did not press the matter. He rolled up beside the boy, and began praising him for his obedience. He complimented him on his manly bearing and spoke flatteringly of his fine pinto pony.

Under the glow of his father's approval, the slow reassuring measures of his voice, John-day lost most of his awe of this strange and powerful man. He had heard Julie tell many times of Snell's wickedness and cruelty, and he had been ashamed to admit even in their closets confidences that the bearded man was his father. Yet from childhood he had learned to respect Snell's strength, his ability to inspire fear in all other men, white or Indian. As a boy he had heard it said that the blood of Cherokees ran in Snell's veins, and that it was this blood which gave him power over other Indians.

John-day's newfound courage led him to tell Snell why he

had been late. "Soldier try follow me," he explained, laughing a little, but as soon as he said it, Snell sprang up and kicked the blazing sticks away from the fire. "You ought to told me that sooner," he said angrily.

"Soldier lost long time back," John-day answered quickly. "Walking soldier. Not know how to ride good."

"You sure?"

Snell now learned that the cavalrymen were all gone from Fort Wicked, Captain Westcott having marched north against the Cheyennes, and this pleased him so that he did not scold the boy further. He also learned that Brad Carlin was very angry because the missionary Metcalfe had come there, and this information pleased Snell even more.

But the news of Fort Wicked that startled him, that was to keep him awake until dawn, was something that came out accidentally—when John-day began boasting of his cattle herd. "John-day have many cattle. More than the warriors. More even than great chief, Wolf Moccasin." When Snell pressed him for details as to how he had acquired these cattle he became reticent, finally admitted he had sworn an oath not to tell how he came by the money to buy his herd.

Snell was puzzled and curious, but he did not urge the boy to reveal the source. And John-day, glowing in unaccustomed man-to-man talk with this giant of a father, supplied the key unknowingly in the rosy complacency of approaching sleep. He told of the excitement of Brad Carlin and Captain Westcott when they discovered he had bought cattle with greenbacks, and how they had suspected him of being mixed up in running whiskey on the reservation. But they got nothing out of him, he said pridefully.

"Greenbacks?" Again Snell felt the startled throb of his heart. He could barely contain himself, yet was afraid to interrupt for fear the boy would stop talking. He did stop, but it was from drowsiness rather than timidity or suspicion. The time was far past midnight now, the fire dead, and the stars wheeling toward dawn. Snell waited until John-day was almost asleep, then leaned close to him, whispering hoarsely: "It was the girl, the one you call Julie, who gave you the saddlebag," he said. "She gave you the greenbacks, too, didn't she?"

"Yes." The boy's eyelids fluttered, then he stared up in fright, realizing he had broken the oath. Fighting sleep, he wondered how the bearded giant could have known this, wondered at his strange power to read other men's thoughts.

"How much money was it?" Snell asked quietly.

"Five hundred dollar. Then another hundred." The boy worried a little because he had broken the oath, then dismissed the worry because he knew the oath could not concern Yankee Snell. The oath concerned only Julie and Agent Carlin and himself, maybe Captain Westcott. But not Snell. Where the money had come from he did not know, and did not care. He slept.

But Snell slept none that night. He rolled restlessly in his blankets, cursing the girl, knowing she must have the stolen payroll hidden somewhere down there at Fort Wicked—giving it away to such as the breed boy—and he was powerless to go and take it from her. He cursed the boy for sleeping so soundly, for using the money to buy cattle, the money that he, Yaneka Snell, had risked his life to take from that Army paymaster.

At first dawn, he kicked John-day roughly awake. The boy was up immediately, reserved and uncommunicative in the reality of morning. Snell shared pemmican and biscuits with him, trying to draw him out, but the boy would say little.

"You're almost a man," Snell said. "Will you go into the tribe?"

John-day's face brightened a little. "Me smoke pipe for sun dance," he answered with pride. "Take vows. Be Arapaho brave."

"Sun dance?" Snell brushed crumbs away from his beard. "So Carlin will permit a sun dance?"

"He has not spoken against it."

"When is it to be?"

"When the moon and dog star rise together."

Snell continued rubbing his beard, rolling the thought of the sun dance around in his mind. On the older reservations, he knew, the sun dance was forbidden. His round eyes enlarged as excitement grew in him.

He spat out the residue of pemmican, and turned to pick up his saddle. "Time for me to be ridin'," he said, almost jovially.

"Me go with you?"

"No. You go back to Fort Wicked." Snell noticed the boy

looked relieved. "Seven days from now, you will bring the missionary, the one who calls himself Metcalfe, to this place." He held up seven fingers. "Seven days."

"And if he will not come?"

"He will come if you say my name, but speak it in a whisper when no one else is nearby. It will go bad for you if you speak my name to anyone—to that girl, or the agent—anyone." Anger showed in his bulging eyes as he continued: "They are enemies of your father."

"John-day say nothing."

"Tell the missionary, Metcalfe, I have big news for him."

"Yes."

With a vicious jerk, Snell tightened his saddle cinch. "Seven days from now, you bring Metcalfe. Start after dark so the soldiers will not see you. You hear?"

"Yes. John-day good boy. Obey father."

Snell mounted, his red lips grinning through his beard, and then he started his horse through the cedars. He did not look back once. He was thinking about the greenbacks. The money was still at Fort Wicked somewhere. The girl, Julie, knew where it was hidden. *And she was the only one who knew.*

* * *

It was after dawn when John-day and Obadiah Metcalfe reached the Twin Buttes—a week after the boy's meeting there with Snell—and from his hiding place in the cedars, the black-bearded man watched the pair riding up the creek. After making certain that no one was following them, he went down to the trail to meet them.

Wasting no time or ceremonies, Snell led them up to his breakfast fire and shared coffee from his tin cup. To be rid of John-day, he ordered the boy to take his horse to the creek for watering. He then turned to Metcalfe and broached the subject that was uppermost in his mind: "I heard the Arapahoes are fixin' for a sun dance."

Metcalfe raised his bleary eyes. "Yes."

"You ever seen a sun dance, Obadiah?"

"No. I hear tell it's a heathenish custom."

"Worse than that, Obadiah." Snell settled down on a flat rock, his large eyes fixed on the missionary. "Sun dances ain't allowed by missionaries on other reservations. The tribes dance naked, bucks and squaws together. It makes 'em drunker'n swiggin' whiskey. By dark they're all out in the bushes." He used a plain word that Metcalfe changed.

"Fornicating," the missionary said, his small eyes glittering. "An abomination."

"They go wild, set up idols and worship 'em, too."

"I shall pray for their souls, Mr. Snell."

Snell shook his head sadly. "It's your duty to do more than pray, Obadiah. The Lord sent you here to civilize these poor heathen from their sinful ways."

The missionary pulled at his long nose, his eyes watering from the fatigue settling on him after the long night ride. "You mean I should forbid the sun dance, Mr. Snell?"

"Like I said, Obadiah, it's your duty."

"Would the Indians obey me? I'm new on the reservation. Few come to hear me preach the word." Metcalfe's voice turned to a whine. "Agent Carlin gives me no assistance or encouragement."

"I warned you Carlin was a black-souled bastard." Snell pressed his advantage, his voice hard and eager: "You listen to me, and we'll soon be shed of Carlin."

"I'm obliged to you for your many kind favors, Mr. Snell."

Snell grinned, his tongue licking out through his beard. "I'm a friend of the Indians." He paused, and then went on: "When you get back to Fort Wicked, you go see the chief, Wolf Moccasin. Tell him the Great White Medicine Chief above has spoken to you. Tell Wolf Moccasin the Great White Medicine Chief will be angry if his Arapaho children hold a sun dance."

As he listened, Metcalfe's thin shoulders straightened under his black sack coat; it was as if he gathered strength and determination from the bearded man's words. "I will do this," he said. "Yes, I will do this."

Snell reached under his blanket and drew out a small liquor flask. "We'll drink on it, Obadiah."

After the missionary had drunk greedily, Snell drawled: "Wolf Moccasin won't like it, of course."

"You mean he won't obey me?" Metcalfe looked alarmed.

"He'll likely go to Carlin." Snell leaned his head back and let the whiskey drain into his throat. He wiped his lips with the back of his hand. "And Carlin, bein' the bastard he is, will side with the Indians."

Metcalfe was shaking his head slowly, his eyes dulling.

"That's when you show you're a fighter for the Lord, Obadiah. There's a telegraph there in the soldier camp. Nobody can stop you usin' it. You send a telegraph to that missionary society and another one to the guv'ment men at Washington and tell 'em Carlin is stoppin' you from the Lord's work. You'll see what happens. They don't like sun dances, them guv'ment people."

John-day was coming back up through the cedars from the creek, leading Snell's horse.

"You're a smart man, Mr. Snell," Metcalfe cried. "And a saintly man, the Lord be praised!"

"You do as I say, Obadiah." Snell lowered his voice so the boy would not hear him. "Say nothin' of this to John-day. But if you need me, go to the boy and tell him to bring you to me. He'll know how to find me."

His weariness and dejection forgotten, Metcalfe stood up, stretching his loose-sleeved arms that were like a crow's wings, almost flapping them in an ecstasy of imagined power, in a dream of shining glory.

11

SERGEANT MARTIN KILFOYLE, COMMANDING THE SIXTEEN infantrymen responsible for the security of Ford Wicked, was a spit-and-polish noncommissioned officer who could have been a lieutenant but for his innate reluctance to accept final responsibility. Kilfoyle's dependability was recognized by every officer he had served under. He could be relied upon to carry out to the letter any order given him. He always saw that his men kept their barracks in apple-pie order, their uniforms neat and clean, their leather burnished, their weapons oiled and ready for inspection.

But the sergeant was uneasy in situations requiring decisions upon his own authority. Since Captain Westcott's sudden departure from the agency, Kilfoyle had been in a continual state of perturbation. Not only was he cut loose from higher command, he was forced into a quasi-military relationship with a civilian who possessed more authority than he—the agent, Brad Carlin. It was not that he distrusted Carlin. He respected the agent and considered him a friend, but he was uncertain as to how the chain of command operated under such a condition. He could find nothing in his infantry manual that covered the situation.

This morning as he rode up the creek he worried over the report he must make to Carlin. The agent obviously had been displeased over the last report—that the soldier assigned to watch John-day had followed the half-breed off the reservation but had then lost the trail. John-day had returned to Fort Wicked before the inept soldier finally gave up and rode back in alone.

When Kilfoyle saw Carlin coming down the trail on his gray

horse, he pulled aside to wait for him. "Morning, Sergeant." The agent's greeting was crisp, but his face bore traces of anxiety.

"Good morning, sir." Kilfoyle pushed his forage cap back over his close-clipped iron-gray hair, wondering if he should delay his report until Carlin was in a brighter mood.

"Any news on your telegraph about Captain Westcott?"

"Yes, sir. The operator at Fort Yellowhorse reports the captain's troop has been ordered back there."

"Might be good news, mightn't it? Perhaps C Troop will be back here soon."

"I hope so," Kilfoyle replied fervently.

"I'd rest easier if they were here for this sun dance. Lots of Greasy Faces are coming in everyday. Have your men keep a sharp lookout and make certain all newcomers are disarmed. Assuring them of course they'll get their weapons back when the sun dance is ended."

Kilfoyle nodded. "I'm seeing to that, sir." He hesitated, then added: "We've found no trace of any whiskey for several days."

"No signs of drunkenness this morning, for sure," Brad said, and forced a grin. "You know, I'm almost convinced one of Westcott's troopers was at the bottom of it. So far as I can tell not a buck's been drunk since the cavalry marched out of here."

"You can be sure none of my infantry boys had any hand in it," Kilfoyle replied earnestly.

"No. They couldn't sit a horse long enough to bring the stuff in." He smiled and changed his tone: "John-day been making any more rides?"

Kilfoyle's freckled face revealed his concern. "He was gone all day yesterday, sir. Must've sneaked out the night before. Private Johansen saw him ride in early this morning."

Brad shook his head. "Did Johansen check what he was carrying?"

"He wasn't carrying anything, sir. Saddlebag almost empty."

"What was the boy's explanation?"

"Same as before. He just went for a ride." Before Brad could reply, Kilfoyle added: "He wasn't alone, sir. The missionary was with him—Metcalfe."

"Hell fire! Did that buzzard have anything to say?"

"He said he went to see some of the country."

Brad gazed off across the creek to where the Arapahoes' smoke-stained lodges dotted the flats. The Indians were re-arranging the tepees in preparation for sun dance ceremonies. "Keep a close watch on that pair, Sergeant. There'll be hell to pay if the bucks mix whiskey with their dancing."

"Yes, sir." The sergeant automatically began a salute, check-ing it in mid-air. "When do you think they'll start—the danc-ing, I mean?"

"Any day now. The braves will fast three or four days, then they'll start the big foofaraw. We can handle it, if we can keep whiskey out." Brad lifted his reins. "Keep me informed, Ser-geant."

When Brad entered his trading store a few minutes later, Julie was at the counter swapping banter with a passing wagon freighter. Her eyes met Brad's for a second, then shifted signifi-cantly toward the fireplace, her mouth making a small grimace of disdain.

Beside the fireplace, Obadiah Metcalfe was taking his ease in the carpet-cloth chair, his head nodding as he dozed. Resenting the man's presence in that particular chair, Brad strode over to him and rapped him sharply on the shoulder. Metcalfe's head rocked back, exposing his corded neck; his eyes blinked open. "Bless me," he cried, "I was just setting here admiring your pretty daughter, Mr. Carlin. Must have dozed off."

"When a man rides around nights, Metcalfe, he gets sleepy daytimes. You want to see me about something?"

The missionary squeezed a thumb and forefinger nervously over the end of his long nose, his bloodshot eyes showing alarm at Brad's reference to his night's journey. He tried to conceal his feelings with a pontifical bow. "Ah, yes, one of our young Arapahoes offered to show me some of the surrounding coun-try. I fear we rode too far."

Brad crossed over and leaned against the counter, staring at Metcalfe until the missionary averted his eyes. "What was on your mind, Mr. Metcalfe?"

"*Reverend* Metcalfe, if you please, sir."

Brad jerked his head down in grudging assent. He was irri-tated by the man's presence, and annoyed with Julie and the wagon driver who were continuing their cozy tête-à-tête in undertones. He waited impatiently for the missionary to state his business.

"I've come to beseech your aid, Mr. Carlin," Metcalfe began, "in the cause which I represent."

"I've already promised that," Brad replied stiffly.

Metcalfe nodded as he continued: "It has come to my attention that the tribe is preparing for a sun dance. This is a pagan ceremony, Mr. Carlin, and cannot be permitted."

Brad sighed. "I know the authorities are opposed to sun dances."

"Yet you have done nothing to stop this one."

"I happen to disagree with the authorities." He smiled patiently. "I believe a man has a right to worship as he chooses."

Metcalfe looked shocked. "Worship?" He clucked his tongue in disapproval. "Surely you don't believe the wild naked dancing of these savages is worship, Mr. Carlin? Their self-tortures, their sinful fornicating—"

"This is not a buffalo dance." Brad's voice turned gruff. "It's a sun dance, a religious ceremony. As for self-tortures, I've forbidden lacerating and skewering. But if some young buck gets worked up enough to scar hisself a bit, I may look the other way."

Metcalfe rose from the chair, his loose black sleeves flapping as he pulled himself erect. "You sorrow me, Mr. Carlin. Your soul is as lost as one of your savages."

"You ever see a sun dance, Reverend?"

"No, and I hope blessed Providence will spare me from ever looking upon such orgies." Metcalfe fixed his bleary eyes on Julie. "Whatever you may think of the Indian dancing, I'd allow your sense of decency would lead you to keep such wantonness from your young daughter. I've heard tell of how the squaws behave, dragging men into the bush for unspeakable debaucheries."

Brad could not restrain a chuckle. "You've got this sun dance mixed up in your mind with one of your own camp meetings, Reverend. I remember back in Kansas, the camp meetings got so free and frolicsome the deacons had to pass a rule to keep women off the grounds between sunset and sunrise." He leaned back against the counter, enjoying Metcalfe's abashed expression. "Those folks were white, not Indians."

"Satan is always at work, Mr. Carlin."

"Well, you needn't worry about Satan interfering with an Arapaho sun dance. I never figured it all out myself, not being Arapaho, but it's religion, all right. The mysteries of life and death, the struggle between good and evil. And paying respect to a Supreme Being. To an Arapaho it's like being born again, his slate wiped clean, a fresh start. They cut loose when it's over because they feel so good, and I don't say the young bucks and maidens don't get the urge to gratify their love for one another." When he looked up and saw Metcalfe's thin face, cold and sharp as a hatchet blade, he stopped. "But I reckon you wouldn't approve of loving, would you, Metcalfe?"

"I pity you, Mr. Carlin, may the Lord forgive you." The missionary folded his arms, and looked out the window. "Then you refuse to order this heathen custom abolished?"

"It's too late to stop this one. By next year, if you've won them to your kind of thinking, I'll put in a word for your kind of camp meeting. No, the braves have taken their vows and begun their fasting already. To stop it now would be like breaking in on one of your church meetings and interrupting you in the middle of a prayer. And in this case, it wouldn't only be a sacrilege, it would be dangerous. We've taken everything away from these people but their religion. If we take that away too soon they might be riled enough to fight us again."

Metcalfe braced his shoulders. "I hoped I wouldn't be forced to battle singlehanded for the Lord, Mr. Carlin. But you leave me no choice. I shall speak to the chief, Wolf Moccasin. If he cannot be persuaded to paths of righteousness, then I must turn to my superiors."

Down at the other end of the counter, the wagon driver was stuffing his purchases inside his shirt. He winked at Julie, and called out: "See you next trip, Brad."

"Sure," Brad said. "Stop by."

The bell jingled as the man went out the door.

Brad looked back to the missionary. "Anything else on your mind, Metcalfe?"

"Should need arise, I may want to use the Army telegraph, Mr. Carlin. Do you have any objections?"

With a slight gesture of annoyance, Brad turned around the counter. "I won't stop you from using it. But I advise you not to try stirring up trouble. Like I said, you better wait till next year, and stop the sun dance *before* it gets started."

Metcalfe sniffed, and pulled his hat down to the top of his shaggy eyebrows. "Duty is duty, Mr. Carlin, and I must be about the Lord's work. Good day, sir." In his odd stalking gait he started toward the door, bowing to Julie, his thin lips breaking over yellow teeth in a sanctimonious smile. She waited until the door closed, then she turned to Brad, moving her shoulders in an exaggerated shudder. "That man," she said. "He makes my skin crawl."

"Yeah," Brad replied.

* * *

One morning later in the week, Julie put on her long green riding habit and rode Brad's gray horse down to the camp circle of the Arapahoes. The circle actually was a great horseshoe of tepees opening toward the rising sun, the lodges arranged by families according to fixed tribal tradition.

Julie did not enter the horseshoe, but halted the gray a few yards outside the entrance, looking in upon the festive whirlpool of colors, sounds, and smells. Brilliant blankets had been slung over lodgepoles, and even more dazzling ones were on the backs of the bustling Indians. Warriors had donned eagle-feathered war bonnets and bright-colored war shirts; squaws were parading the gayest beaded dresses. Smells of sage smoke and boiling meat, of horse dung and rawhide, mingled with the tangy air of late summer turning to autumn. And over all ran a babble of sound—excited voices, shrill cries of children, frenetic barking of dogs.

Down in the center of the horseshoe were three secret tepees of preparation, an island of solemnity in the swirl of gaiety. There were quartered the medicine men, warriors who had made vows of thankfulness, and the young men who were to become braves. Around each of these three tepees the ground was covered with a ring of sacred white sage.

Julie knew that John-day was in one of these secret tepees, and she held the gray horse so that she could be plainly seen from anyone of them. After waiting patiently for half an hour, she saw John-day coming toward her.

Except for a breechclout and wreaths of sage and willow around his neck, wrist, and ankles, he was naked. His body was daubed with ochre and vermillion, his face streaked with horizontal lines of black. She would not have known him but for the shield he carried. It was the largest shield of any of the candidates, its size representing his cattle herd, he had explained. It was covered with soft-dressed elkskin and decorated with hairs taken from the tail of his pinto pony.

As he rushed up beside Julie's horse, his eyes were wide with exhilaration, and she could see the beating of his heart beneath his naked painted breast.

"Julie have mirror?" He was panting for breath.

She drew the mirror, wrapped in a cloth, from the pocket of her riding habit, and as she handed it to him it flashed in the morning sun.

"Is fine big mirror!" he cried.

"The largest the peddler man had," Julie said.

He pressed the mirror against his shield. "It will blind the eyes of my enemies," he shouted exultantly in Arapaho. "It will clear the air of evil spirits!"

"You will dance the sun dance with this shield over your shoulder?"

"Ahe-e-ye!" He was lightheaded from his fasting and from the intoxication of the rituals. He chanted in Arapaho: "We shall dance until daylight and our father, the moon, will take pity on us!"

She smiled down at him.

"John-day go now," he said soberly. "Soon go to hills for great lodgepole." He pointed toward the eastern slope where deep green pines formed a sweep into the basin. Then he turned and trotted back into the horseshoe, his mirror flashing as he ran.

That afternoon Julie returned to the camp circle, fascinated by the air of expectancy, the mounting excitement of the Indians. With a loud shaking of rattles and beating of drums, medicine men were going through the camp announcing that it was time to journey to the mountain for the sacred center pole of the great dancing lodge.

From out of the secret tepees of preparation, the painted dancers formed into a marching line behind the medicine men and the chief, Wolf Moccasin. The old chief, bedecked in his trailing headdress of many feathers, led the way, looking neither to right nor left, at first walking slowly, then gradually quickening his pace with the rising beat of the drum. Beside him was the head medicine man, older even than the chief, carrying the tribe's sacred pipe above his head.

After they passed Julie, after the squaws and children had scattered along behind the marchers, she followed slowly at the rear of the procession. She rode all the way to the bottom of the pine-clad slope, dismounting there, and listening to the crack of axes against a tall lodgepole somewhere in the woods above.

When she heard the party returning, she drew the gray horse off a short distance, waiting until she saw the pole bearers break out of the woods. Behind the bearers came the others, burdened with branches of pine needles and other evergreens, walking in a slow purposeful rhythm.

Julie headed straight toward the creek, crossing near the infantry quarters, and returning to the camp circle. The entrance was thronged with squaws and excited children, and there was no room to stand her horse. Turning back until she found a sapling, she fastened the horse and rejoined the crowd.

In a moment she was enveloped by Arapahoes, swaying forward then backward with the crowd as the pole bearers approached. Somewhere inside the tepee ellipse an old man began beating a small drum, and the squaws set up a discordant singsong.

As soon as the dancers reached the designated site of the great sun-dance lodge, the throng swept after them, and Julie found herself caught in the surging mass. She resisted, trying to break out of the stream of chanting Indians, but it was useless. After a minute or so she found herself on the inner circle of the crowd. In the open space before her a medicine man was painting the lodgepole with red and black stripes, another was decorating it with scarlet squaw cloth. When they finished their work, the chief medicine man brought forth a buffalo skull and a blackened rawhide which had been cut into the figure of a mounted warrior. Two braves fastened these objects to the top of the pole and as the crowd cried out its approval, the raisers took their places, planting the tall pole in the deep hole already prepared for it.

Suddenly from out of the group of dancers, a single arrow streaked skyward, penetrating the figure of the blackened warrior. The rawhide image swayed back and forth, alternately caught in the late afternoon sunlight, then silhouetted against the azure sky.

For a moment the watchers were silent; then a babble of voices broke the stillness, the crowd dissolving slowly, as if reluctantly. Like a colony of ants, each with an appointed task, the Arapahoes began the work of completing the great lodge, planting shorter poles around the tall center one, joining the rafters, and covering all except the opening with evergreens.

As Julie walked slowly toward the horseshoe's entrance, she was aware that the Indians were watching her closely, but she decided it was best to speak to no one, not even to those she knew by name. She looked back once at the tall pole; the buffalo skull and the rawhide figure were like black carvings against the sinking sun.

When she started out the opening, she almost collided with Obadiah Metcalfe.

He had a wild, frantic gleam in his eyes. "Sin and perdition," he muttered, his hand clutching at the girl's shoulder. "Perish this day, for the eyes of an innocent maiden are made unclean by these heathen iniquities! Allow me to pray for you, miss." His fingers squeezed into her flesh.

She squirmed away from him, running toward her picketed horse. She did not look back until she was in the saddle. As if he had forgotten her, the missionary was still standing in the entrance of the camp circle, his hands clasped over his coattails, his long nose pointed toward the top of the great lodgepole.

After watching Metcalfe for a moment, Julie started in the direction of the trading store. When she cut into the trail she heard a horse trotting up from the infantry camp, and glancing back, recognized Sergeant Kilfoyle. She held the gray until the sergeant came alongside.

He nodded and smiled, but his freckled face quickly turned grave. "You should not be riding about alone, miss," he said. "Not after sunset leastwise."

"What on earth do you mean, Sergeant Kilfoyle?" She pulled the gray in toward the hitching rail.

"It's not safe, Miss Julie. Some bad signs of trouble brewing. I've come to warn Mr. Carlin."

They found Brad in the back of the store unpacking a crate,

and the sergeant immediately handed him a folded sheet of telegrapher's paper. "Metcalfe sent this message out sometime this afternoon, sir. The signal corporal couldn't find me—I was up on the north range at the time—or I'd never have let it pass."

"I told Metcalfe he could use the telegraph," Brad said.

"That's what he informed the corporal." Kilfoyle looked as if he did not believe what he had just heard.

"But I warned him not to try and stir up things." Brad unfolded the paper and went over to the window to read it. As he read, he swore once or twice under his breath. "Well, this'll likely rimrock me for good. The buzzard don't say outright that I'm a devil with horns, but anybody that didn't know me would sure think so." He grinned cheerfully at the sergeant. "Time's on our side, Kilfoyle. Before the bureau cracks its big whip at me, that sun dance may be over, anyway."

"Something else you ought to know, sir. Several visiting parties came in this afternoon, acted ugly when my men took their weapons. They had whiskey."

"Greasy Faces?"

"Mostly."

"That's bad. And you with only sixteen men. What a hell of a time for Ben Westcott to be off chasing Cheyennes."

12

AT THAT MOMENT, HOWEVER, CAPTAIN WESTCOTT WAS NOT pursuing Cheyennes. Resistance from the hostiles had collapsed, Colonel Comstock's field battalion had gone into camp north of Goldfield, and C Troop was back in Fort Yellowhorse. Horses had been reshod, and the men, recuperated from forced marches, were already beginning to suffer a new weariness—the tedium of garrison duties.

Westcott was in his comfortable room in bachelor officers' quarters, pondering a letter he had received late that day from Peter Dunreath, who had been scouting all summer with Comstock's battalion. The letter was scrawled on a piece of wrapping paper:

Ben Westcott, capt.
Figgered I oughta let you know a bout somethin I lerned in Goldfield Sat. night when I was ther with sum of the boys. Saw old Domino Ruark in the Troopers Rest, and you wont beleeve this, Domino said he saw Yankee Snell in town. You know old Domino is not one to big talk and he would know Snell, all right. I did some nosin round mongst the buffalo boys and found out more. Yankee Snell is sum where round these parts for sure. The word is he was buyin whiskey and stolen army guns. Thot you oughta know. Will keep my eyes and ears peel back—let you know what I can find out. Nothing worth a damn going on here. Wish I was back with the C troop boys.

Yrs. obed.
P. Dunreath

As Westcott read and reread the letter, old and bitter memories surged within him. Long ago he had accepted the fact that Yaneka Snell was dead, and with that acceptance, hate had drained away from him. And his love for Julie, he knew, had all but obliterated the ancient scars left by the memory of Anna Llewellyn.

But it was not so much the old hatred that troubled him now, it was apprehension. What was Snell doing in Goldfield? Was he operating his nefarious trading schemes in the Cheyenne country? Or could he possibly be involved farther south, running liquor into Fort Wicked, perhaps? *The greenbacks!* John-day's mysterious greenbacks! Could there be a connection with the Army payroll Snell had stolen and which had never been recovered? He dismissed the thought as being fantastic, yet it kept coming back, uneasily in his mind.

Restless and troubled, Westcott went out for a walk around the old stockade, climbed to the north parapet and watched the river running like a sheet of metal under the stars. After tattoo sounded, he walked briskly back to his quarters, resolved that early on the morrow he would call upon the commanding officer and urge him to speed the expected orders returning Troop C to Fort Wicked.

13

SERGEANT MARTIN KILFOYLE SAT BEFORE A ROUGH PINE-board desk in the infantry orderly room at Fort Wicked, puzzling over a telegraph message which had just been brought to him by the signal corporal. The message had originated from Headquarters Department of the Platte, relayed *via* Fort Laramie. It directed the Commanding Officer, Arapaho Springs Agency, to cooperate with Reverend Obadiah Metcalfe in prohibiting sun dance ceremonies pursuant to official regulations, by order of the Commanding General.

Kilfoyle had already searched his manuals for guidance, and knew there was nothing in any of them concerning sun dances. He was further troubled by the salutation "Commanding Officer, Arapaho Springs Agency," and the awesome closing phrase, "by order of the Commanding General."

After mulling over the contents of the message for several minutes, he went outside, mounted his horse, and rode up to see Brad Carlin.

"What frets me," Kilfoyle said, after Brad had read the telegram, "is the order didn't come from Yellowhorse. That's where I make my reports, sir."

Brad gave the sergeant a stogie, and lit one himself. "Could be they couldn't get through to Fort Yellowhorse."

"Yeah, the crazy Cheyennes always cutting the wires around there." Kilfoyle chewed nervously on the cigar. "Devil take it, Mr. Carlin, do I have to go to that Metcalfe and ask *him* what he wants me to do?"

"Hell fire no, not yet awhile." Brad blew out a swirl of smoke. "We got to stall for time. The Indians been dancing two days now and we've had no trouble. Two more days and they're done. They haven't started in yet today, have they?"

"Quiet as a whisper when I left, sir. I reckon they're still sleeping off last night's ruckus."

"Metcalfe been around warning 'em again?"

"He's always around," Kilfoyle replied gloomily.

Brad reached for his hat. "Let's go down to your telegraph and see if we can get through to Fort Yellowhorse. If Captain Westcott is there, maybe he can stall off that headquarters order a couple of days. Then it won't matter."

But the signal corporal was unable to rouse the Yellowhorse operator. He tapped away at his key, finally gave up, and ventured an opinion that the wire had either been cut by the hostiles, or fouled by a storm or some prowling animal.

"If Metcalfe comes around," Brad warned the corporal, "keep your lips shut. Tell him nothing. And keep trying to reach Fort Yellowhorse." He turned to Kilfoyle. "The way the drums are beating over there, the dancers must be starting up again. Let's go have a look."

After they had mounted and started across the creek, Kilfoyle spoke up: "I don't feel right about this, Mr. Carlin. You see, I'm acting as commanding officer here, and the commanding general has given me an order. I ought to carry it out."

Brad had lifted his legs to avoid the splashing water. When the gray stepped ashore, he set his boots back in the stirrups, and replied quietly: "If Metcalfe don't ask you to do nothing, you don't have to do nothing. We'll keep shy of that missionary till the dancing is all done. Let's just hope he don't try anything rash."

Hitching their mounts outside the tepee ellipse, they walked down to the sun-dance lodge and squatted cross-legged at one side of the entrance. The air smelled of sage and drying pine needles. Inside, filtered sunlight fell over the drummers around their large skin drum. They were chanting a weird unmelodic hymn. In the background a ring of squaws added a discordant singsong, broken by sudden shouts and shrieks.

When the preliminaries ended, the dancers entered—fifty or more freshly painted braves and young men wearing breechclouts and sage wreaths. Each dancer carried in his mouth a whistle made of an eagle's wing or the bone of a crane's leg mounted with eagle down. After forming part of a circle around the tall center pole, they threw their heads back, fixing their eyes trancelike upon the high buffalo skull and the rawhide figure of the naked warrior. They danced toward the pole, then backward, then forward again, blowing their bone whistles in shrill overtones to the monotonous tom-tom beat of the drum and the guttural chant of the medicine men.

"How they keep that up hour after hour beats me," Kilfoyle commented in a hoarse whisper.

"Maybe they wonder how your infantry boys can march all day and all night, hour after hour," Brad replied dryly. He glanced at his watch. "Looks peaceful enough in there. And no sign of Metcalfe around anywhere. Let's go back and see if that corporal's got through to Fort Yellowhorse."

* * *

It was late afternoon when they finally gave up trying to reach the Yellowhorse telegraph operator. Kilfoyle had just suggested that Brad stay around and take evening mess with his squad, when they heard a horse's hoofs beating outside. "Brad, Brad, Brad!" It was Julie's voice, calling out of fear and desperation. When Brad flung the barracks door open, he saw her galloping toward him. She was riding bareback on John-day's pinto pony.

"Brad, for God's sake, come quick!"

He ran forward, catching at the pinto's rope bridle. "What's the matter, girl?"

"It's Metcalfe." Her violet eyes dilated with excitement. "He's got an ax. They'll kill him if you don't hurry."

"Where is he?"

"At the sun-dance lodge. He's jabbering like a crazy man. He tried to cut the lodgepole!"

Kilfoyle's boots banged on the barracks steps, his voice bellowing orders. Infantrymen in various stages of dress clattered out of the building with their rifles, falling into formation. There were only ten of them, the others being on mounted guard duty around the agency.

Brad turned back to Julie, his face drained of color. "You get back up to the store fast, girl, and lock yourself in. Hear me?"

She nodded, but made no move to go.

"Hurry up!" Brad slapped the pinto's rump, and she turned the pony up the trail toward the trading store, glancing back fearfully over her shoulder.

Kilfoyle had stopped barking his orders, and was looking questioningly at Brad.

"Where'n hell are your mounts?" Brad asked.

"In the corral, sir. I can double-time the men over there quicker'n we can get saddles and bridles on."

Brad jumped astride the gray, and wheeled. "All right, get to it! I'll ride ahead." As he plunged across the creek, he could hear Kilfoyle's command: "At the double!"

Galloping hard, he shot straight through the eastern opening of the tepee ellipse, and did not slow his mount until he reached the milling circle of Indians before the sun-dance lodge. He motioned the crowd to open, and forced the gray through to the center.

Like some outraged animal, Metcalfe stood besieged upon a stump, ax in hand, mouthing condemnations mixed with incongruous scriptural phrases. The whole effect of his tirade bordered on blasphemy. To Brad Carlin the spectacle signaled danger as acute as that of a blazing bonfire let loose in the midst of a tinder-dry forest.

Many of the Arapahoes had turned their attention to the agent who had appeared so suddenly among them, and Brad scanned their faces, trying to read what might be written upon those usually inscrutable countenances. If any emotion showed there, it was incomprehension mixed with disbelief. But he knew anger was smoldering beneath, and it could erupt at any second.

Wolf Moccasin and one of the older medicine men pushed through the crowd. Several dancers fell in behind their leaders, and then as suddenly as a wind shifts during a storm, Brad became the center of the swirling mass of Indians.

Still wearing his trailing headdress, Wolf Moccasin halted before the agent's gray horse. He began speaking in Arapaho, his deep voice rising and falling. Either he was too wrought up to use the few English words he knew, or was deliberately refusing to use them. As well as Brad could make out, he was accusing the "blackcoat man, Metcalfe" of defiling the sun-dance lodge.

Before Brad could reply, he heard Kilfoyle's infantrymen coming, their double-time steps like oddly paced hoofbeats on the hard-packed earth.

Exactly what happened during the next two or three minutes was never clear to Brad. Nor was Kilfoyle, in reconstructing the swift events, ever certain, either. Brad recalled that most of the members of the milling throng of Indians had turned their attention to the armed soldiers. Yet some of them—mostly a few squaws near the great tepee's entrance—also were watching what Metcalfe was doing.

In the distraction of Brad's arrival and the successive confusion of the onrushing foot soldiers, Metcalfe somehow had made his way into the lodge, and with frenzied strokes of his ax was attacking the symbolic center pole.

From his saddle, Brad could see only flashes of motion, a flying chip of wood, a half-naked dancer flinging himself upon the missionary, the gleam of the steel ax blade. He yelled to Sergeant Kilfoyle, but the soldiers were already beating their way into the lodge, using rifle butts as clubs. Screams and wild shouts, the high singsong cry of a medicine man, the gibbering voice of Obadiah Metcalfe—all filled the air.

In a minute, Kilfoyle's men were coming back outside, still fighting against a crowd torn by emotions of anger and fear. A rifle shot cracked from somewhere, and then suddenly the soldiers were in the open, formed in a hollow square around the black-coated figure of Metcalfe, whose arms were flailing wildly as they forced him along. He no longer had his ax, and one of his sleeves was ripped from wrist to shoulder.

Quickly, Brad closed in behind the tiny square of soldiers, turning his horse and facing back upon the crowd. "Go back to your dancing!" he shouted, and noticed for the first time that the great pole of the dance lodge leaned askew, its buffalo skull and the warrior figure hanging at opposite angles against the twilight sky.

Wolf Moccasin broke out of the crowd, his headdress shaking furiously. His face was dark with anger and hatred. "Give us the blackcoat man!" he cried in Arapaho.

A brave whom Brad recognized as Red Willow, one of the leaders of the young men, appeared from behind the chief. Drawing his knife, Red Willow dashed toward the soldiers, veering to avoid Brad's horse. Kilfoyle stepped forward, barring the Indian's passage, rifle pointed at his belly.

Brad spoke loudly, struggling to hold his voice calm: "Go back, Red Willow." The brave looked up at him, hesitating a moment while the agent continued: "The blackcoat missionary is under arrest. He will receive white man's justice. I promise."

Red Willow held his ground, his eyes turning back to Kilfoyle. But he sheathed his knife.

"Let's go," Brad said to Kilfoyle. "Up to my place."

By the time the soldiers reached the trading store, twilight was deepening to darkness. The front door was barred on the inside, and Brad had to knock loudly before Julie came to open it. Her face looked pale in the light of the oil lamp she carried. Brad took the lamp and drew her out of the way as he beckoned the soldiers to bring Metcalfe inside.

"Put him in the back storage room," he said wearily, and ignored Metcalfe's vehement protests while the soldiers were forcing the missionary through the inner door. When they closed it upon him, Brad went over and shoved the heavy wooden latch into place. "No windows in there," he said to Kilfoyle "He'll be cosy enough."

Julie was tugging at his elbow. "That telegraph operator was up here a minute ago," she said hurriedly. "He wanted me to tell you the line was open to Fort Yellowhorse."

"Yes?" The tension in his face relaxed slightly. "Well, that's the first *good* news I've heard today." His voice sobered as he looked at Kilfoyle. "But it may be too late now." As if regretting the last remark, he patted Julie's shoulder reassuringly. "Sergeant, you'd better put a message through immediately to Fort Yellowhorse. Tell them we're in trouble. We need a cavalry troop as fast as they can send one."

14

A SHORT TIME AFTER THE WARNING TELEGRAM HAD COME
from Sergeant Kilfoyle, Captain Westcott was leading Troop C
out of Fort Yellowhorse, following the telegraph line straight
south across the grasslands. At the first nooning stop, he ordered his signalman to connect the portable telegraph into the
wire and was reassured to learn that all was quiet among the
Indians on the agency. The missionary, Metcalfe, was still being
held under military arrest.

Ordinarily an overland march from Fort Yellowhorse to Fort
Wicked required almost a week, but by mid-morning of the
fourth day, C Troop was entering Clear Creek ravine, within a
few hours' easy reach of the Arapaho agency.

This morning, however, the signal corporal had been unable
to establish communication with Fort Wicked. Westcott was
disturbed by this, but after a look at the rotting cottonwood
poles and rusting wire in that section of the line, he was inclined
to accept the philosophical comment of the signalman that it
was a miracle any dot or dash could carry over such equipment.

Yet now, as he led C Troop along Clear Creek and into the
deepening ravine, his vague anxiety persisted. Not only was the
telegraph wire dead, his forward scouts were reporting signs of
Indians ahead. Added to this was the weariness of his men and
horses. The past two days they had marched from seven in the
morning until near midnight each day; this morning he had set
them moving before dawn.

He attempted to blame his gnawing uneasiness on bitter
memories of Clear Creek ravine. It was here that Yaneka Snell
and the renegade Arapahoes had raided the wagon train; it was
here on that bright summer day they had killed Anna Llewel-

lyn. His long-buried hatred of Snell rose again like the cruel
aching of an old wound. But his main concern was uncertainty
over what was happening at Fort Wicked. He worried over the
safety of Julie. He knew her impetuousness, her wild disregard
for physical danger. He thought of the Arapahoes, how close
they were actually to being blanket Indians—with their long
heritage of violence and their distrust of the white man. They
had been badly used by that missionary and whoever it was that
had been supplying the young bucks with whiskey. Again he
was reminded of Snell, his anger sharp against frustrations of
time and space.

In the winding, narrowing trail ahead, he saw Sergeant Connors riding back toward him at a fast trot. He quickened the
pace of his own mount, leaving the plodding column behind.

"Indians ahead, sir!" Connors shouted. "Arapahoes, I figger."

"How many?" Westcott tugged at his reins, halting beside the
sergeant.

"Saw only three. Had their heads up over some rocks. When
I waved they just disappeared."

"Where're the scouts?"

"I told 'em to hold their position till I reported to you, sir."

Westcott turned and raised his gauntlet in a signal to Lieutenant Jackson who was halfway back in the column. "Let's go up
and have a look."

The scouts were waiting, just off the trail, in attitudes of
wariness. "We saw 'em again, sir," one trooper said. "Dozen or
more lurkin' about down there." He pointed at a rock outcrop-
ping three hundred yards ahead.

Westcott removed his hat, his red hair tumbling over his ears
and forehead. "Keep closed up and follow me." Waving his hat
from side to side, he advanced slowly. The canyon widened, the
small creek shooting off in a spray of rapids through jagged
stones, the trail cutting through a level patch of high dry grass
and sagebrush.

Suddenly out of the grass, the Indians appeared—three of
them, waving bright-colored blankets. One stood a few paces
forward of the others, holding his hand extended, palm outward, moving it sharply to the front and downward.

"Hold it," Westcott said quietly, reining his mount.

The Indian made the sign for council, and Westcott acknowl-
edged it. "We talk," he said loudly. "Bluecoats friends." He
turned and looked back. The column was moving into the patch
of brown grass. He signaled the lieutenant to halt.

"Go back to Lieutenant Jackson," Westcott said quietly to
Connors, "and tell him to make it look like a rest stop. Some
saddles off, and start rubbing down the mounts. But every man
keep carbines ready and cartridge belts tight. Look sharp
about!"

Dismounting, Westcott walked slowly toward the Indians. By
the time he was within ten yards of them, Wolf Moccasin appeared out of the farther rocks. Beside the chief walked a brave
whom Westcott knew as one of the agency's young leaders, Red
Willow. He was wearing a set of false teeth as a necklace.

After exchanging formal greetings, Westcott asked pointedly:
"Why is my friend, Wolf Moccasin, not on the reservation of his
people? Why is he so far from his lodges?"

Wolf Moccasin folded his arms, and stood with his bowed
legs outspread. In Arapaho, he told of how the blackcoat missionary, Metcalfe, had mocked his people and their religion. He
said Metcalfe was an excrement-eating dog.

Westcott got the meaning of the latter, but understood very
little else. He missed Peter Dunreath; the scout could always
catch the subtleties of the Indian tongues. "Speak in white
man's words," he said, keeping his tone friendly. "Our com-
rade, the scout Dunreath, is not here to tell me what you say."

With a shrug, Wolf Moccasin repeated his tirade in broken
English, and added: "My braves say soldier-chief Westcott
come. Say no want more soldiers on reservation."

Red Willow drew his blanket tight over his shoulders and
stepped in front of the chief. "Is so. No more soldiers. Brother
to Red Willow hurt bad when walking soldiers take blackcoat
man from us. If brother to Red Willow die, blackcoat missionary and one walking soldier must die."

The chief nodded, his eyes searching Westcott's face.

"Let us parley," Westcott said, and asked the scouts to bring
blankets from their horses. In an undertone, he added: "One of
you men go back and bring up some coffee and hardtack."

He motioned the Indians to be seated on the blankets. When
he offered tobacco, they refused it, and he knew that was a bad

sign. If an Indian refused to smoke in council, he was not friendly.

Up the ravine, two or three coffee fires were already smoking. Some of the men were rubbing their mounts down with dry grass. A few horses, released of their loads, were kicking and rolling on the ground.

Westcott thrust his tobacco pouch back in his blouse, and sat down cross-legged, facing the two Arapahoes. Behind them in the trail a dozen or more warriors were watching the proceedings closely. They made no effort to conceal their rifles. The weapons were new. *Remingtons,* Westcott guessed. *A shipment had been reported stolen hear Goldfield. And Yaneka Snell had been there, not long after.*

He spoke slowly, cautiously: "Some Indians good, some Indians bad. Some white men good, some white men bad. White man's justice will decide how to punish the bad missionary."

Wolf Moccasin waved his hand as if brushing Westcott's words away. "What bluecoats come for?" he demanded. His tone was unfriendly.

"We heard the missionary, Metcalfe, was not treating you right. Soldier-chief Westcott, old friend. Come see what big trouble is. Make things good and right again for Wolf Moccasin's people."

One of the scouts arrived with a pot of coffee and some tin cups. He handed Westcott a pack of hardtack, and filled the cups. Westcott passed the hardtack to the two Arapahoes and waited until they lifted their cups before he tasted his coffee. The liquid was barely warm, but it smelled good in the cold shade of the ravine.

Wolf Moccasin licked crumb flecks off his palms, then stared boldly at the captain. "Better stop here," he said harshly.

Westcott held the chief's steady gaze. He knew suddenly that Wolf Moccasin was not interested in discussing anything; the chief was merely bargaining for time. Delay. For what purpose, Westcott could only guess, but he knew he could sit talking through the morning and get nowhere. And Fort Wicked was hours away.

He turned and saw that Sergeant Connors had returned. "Saddle 'em up, Sergeant," he said crisply. "Damn quick."

"Better stop here," Wolf Moccasin repeated warningly.

Connors was already shouting commands.

"You can see there's no fit grass here for my horses," West-cott replied impatiently.

"Go back," Red Willow said, his copper skin tightening over the sharp bones of his face.

Westcott stood up, tossing his blanket to one of the scouts. "I shall march to the big creek in the basin where grass is still green." He added in a conciliatory tone: "Perhaps we can talk again there."

Wolf Moccasin shook his head angrily. He was awkward getting up off the blanket, his muscles reluctant against his old bones. With his index finger he signaled the warrior in the trail to bring his horse.

By the time C Troop was mounted and ready to march, the Arapahoes had vanished.

After the column was in motion, Westcott joined Connors in the advance. "Them warriors up in the trail, sir," Connors said worriedly, "they seemed mighty interested in our horses."

"They were counting the troop," Westcott replied. "I suppose I should have held the chief as hostage till we reach Fort Wicked."

The sergeant glanced up over his head at the towering bluffs. "I feel better now we're movin' out of here, sir. They could roll rocks right down on our heads."

As soon as the trail straightened, the column struck a slow trot and held it for a mile. Westcott kept thirty yards ahead of the troop, and when the canyon widened and the hills lowered and fell away on either side, he threw out advance guards on the flanks. To impress any watching Indians, he ordered the guidon bearer to unfurl the swallow-tailed color and set it flapping in the stiff breeze from the west.

He had just slackened speed to a walk when he saw one of the forward scouts circling his horse and beckoning. Westcott turned in his saddle, shouting back to Lieutenant Jackson: "At a gallop!"

As he came down on the waiting scout, he saw an overturned wagon fifty yards ahead. He halted until the column closed up, ordering a cautious approach in spreading files without riders on the ridges, but there was no sign of Indians in the vicinity. Six dead mules lay stretched about the wagon. What was left of two white men were flung beside the angled bed—scalped, stripped, and partially burned.

"Mr. Jackson, dismount the men and reset saddles!"

"Shall we bury the wagoners, sir?"

"No time for that now." Westcott's eyes, half-closed against the brilliant autumn sun, scanned the slopes around. "God save our horses, but we're going for Fort Wicked at all speed possible."

Jackson shouted an order to the sergeants, and dismounted beside Westcott. "They've gone back to the blanket with a vengeance, wouldn't you say so, sir?"

"That's putting it mildly." Behind him came the rustle and rattle of the dismounting troop.

From the overturned wagon and its dead, the trail sloped for a mile to a shallow ford. At that point was the juncture with the main route south to Fort Wicked, and once they were on that level trail they could ride hard and fast. Three—maybe four—hours would do it. But he wondered if it was not already too late.

Resuming march, they faced into a wind that ruffled the dry grass and sagebrush on either side of them. In some places high brown tufts folded over into the narrow trail, beating against the riders' booted legs. Westcott kept flankers well out to right and left now, scouring the slopes. He held the pace to a slow trot, conserving the horses' remaining strength for the final dash he intended to begin as soon as they were into the basin.

At last he saw the shiny, wide-flowing creek like a bordering ribbon at the end of the grass. A thicket of yellow aspens marked the farther side of the familiar crossing.

Dropping back, he ordered the trumpeter to bugle in the outriders, and as these troopers worked their way down through the sagebrush, he passed an order back. They would cross by platoons, keeping thirty yards apart, and as they entered the main trail would form twos and break into a gallop.

Westcott rode at the head of the first platoon, setting the pace as they came down into the sandy approach. His horse had scarcely wet its fetlocks when a rifle cracked, followed by a scattering of fire. His mount reared, whinnying with pain, and as the animal wheeled, a riderless horse dashed into view—one of the forward scouts'. The flapping rein, the dangling stirrups,

the blanket roll at the pommel dripping with blood—all revealed the story. Another trooper fell, just behind Westcott,
sliding off his saddle into the stream.

He ordered the platoon to fall back on the column, dismounting the men quickly and forming a skirmish line. But no
attack came.

The trooper who had fallen into the creek still lay there, the
awkward sprawl of his body in the shallows telling plainly
enough that he was beyond the need of medical aid. Westcott's
horse had received a slight flesh wound across one shoulder,
and three or four other mounts had been hit. One was down in
the trail.

Westcott turned to Sergeant Connors. "They're in behind
that aspen thicket across the creek. We need to know how
many. Mount and take a set of fours to the left and get up on
that ridge over there. If you can see them, wave your hat, and
hold until I can come up."

Except for the movements of the horse holders in the rear
and the fading hoofbeats of Connors' reconnaissance party, the
land was silent. Nothing showed in the yellow aspen thicket.
The troop might have been alone, unobserved, performing a
routine field exercise.

After a few minutes Connors vanished over the ridgetop,
then reappeared, silhouetted against the sky, spiraling his hat
above his head. Westcott sprang into his saddle, forcing his
nervous mount up the slope. The summit was rough, strewn
with copper-colored boulders, and he let the horse pick its way
to the sergeant's position.

Connors' usually cheerful face was grave. "If the captain will
dismount, sir, and come with me to that point of rock there—"

"You can see them?" Westcott swung down, handing his
reins to one of the four waiting troopers.

"Thick as flies in a honey pot, sir."

Westcott followed the sergeant toward a mass of broken
rocks, stooping when Connors did, and then crawling after him
to a wind-twisted juniper. Below them lay the brown basin, the
streak of creek with its strip of trail beside it, and off to the right
the splash of yellow thicket by the ford. Up a flat draw, not
more than a mile beyond the thicket, was a tepee village,
crowded between a brook and a slash of dark green pines. All

this, Westcott's eyes swept across in a second. But when he unslung his field glass he fixed it on the aspen thicket. There among the brush and rocks lay the ambush, Indians packed close, for four hundred yards along.

"A good third of the reservation is down there," Westcott declared as he cased his glass. "If you include squaws who must be in those lodges, maybe more than a third."

Connors had been peering off to the south, across the successive folds of hills to the coppery buttes miles away. "Looks like another third may be over there, sir," he said grimly.

Following the direction of the sergeant's outflung gauntlet, Westcott saw three Indians riding over the crest of the nearest ridge. They appeared to be in no hurry, were sauntering in fact, the leader skewed in his saddle in the sort of slouch that was deceptive, Westcott knew, to green West Point cavalry subalterns who had been taught that a proper seat was the first essential to good horsemanship. The lead Indian halted, one hand balancing rifle across saddle, the other shielding his eyes; the fringe of his hunting shirt shaded his face.

"Let's get back to our horses," Westcott said quickly, and added as if thinking aloud: "I'll move the troop up on this ridge."

As he approached the four waiting men, he ordered them to mount, and had barely swung into his saddle when rifle fire crackled, echoing back against the hills. One of the troopers cried out; his horse was down not ten feet off from Westcott, its legs thrashing convulsively.

Westcott sucked in his breath sharply. The rim of the ridge beyond the three sauntering Indian horsemen was lined with warriors. He swung over to the unhorsed trooper, catching his hand and lifting him behind his saddle. The man was unhurt, only astonished.

"Good God Almighty!" Connors shouted, and at first Westcott thought the cry was the sergeant's reaction to the Indians on the ridge. But Connors was staring in the opposite direction, at the ford below. Down there a dozen Arapahoes had crossed the creek on foot and were scurrying like rabbits into the high grass. Puffs of blue smoke rose in their tracks, changing quickly into spurts of flame. The warriors flung their torches ahead of them, and as fire and smoke boiled up, were concealed by it.

Fanned by the steady wind from the basin, the grass fire quickly became a river of flame, swirling toward C Troop—which was dismounted, with horses corralled in the rear.

Westcott gave no order. He hesitated only long enough to dump the trooper off from behind his saddle, then spurred his horse, turning its nose toward the rear of the column. As he thundered down, praying that his mount would not stumble, he could hear Lieutenant Jackson shouting orders. The horse herd was milling, panicked by the smoke.

He had his match block in his hand when he hit the ground, letting his mount run on beyond, and he swore as the first match failed. He made torches of wadded grass, passing them to the horse holders who quickly enough understood what he was doing. C Troop was now blocked front and rear by raging flames and smoke choking lungs and blinding eyes. But as soon as grass and sagebrush burned away in the rear—the wind driving its main fury away from them—the men moved into the cleared and blackened areas, stamping out remnants of fire.

Westcott found Jackson and Connors, and they began forming a skirmish line in the stifling smoke. They could hear the Indians coming before they saw them, their shrill war whoops doubly terrifying because the criers were unseen. The men in the skirmish line coughed, and rubbed knuckles into their eyes. In front of them the last flames shot skyward, vanishing as if cut off from the ground by a giant knife.

Black smoke thinned to a bluish curtain, and then Westcott saw them as in a dream of hell—a few mounted ones in the lead, brandishing weapons, and behind them a wave on foot chattering like birds, knives naked in their hands.

He shouted commands automatically, leveling his own carbine at one of the riders coming headlong, and knocked him off his pony. Carbines rattled furiously all along the skirmish line.

Obviously the Arapahoes had expected the cavalrymen to be disorganized and confused by the grass fire; now it was they who were completely surprised to find an unwavering line awaiting them. After their first assault, they rallied only long enough to recover their casualties, then withdrew rapidly, running for cover of the thicket across the creek.

Westcott took a quick look around him. Knots of grass still burned all about, but high wind thinned the smoke, and most of the troopers had stopped their coughing. The backfire was blazing itself out up in the ravine.

Lieutenant Jackson came up, limping slightly, his smudged face grinning with relief. "Shall we mount and head for high ground, sir?"

"Take a look at the high ground, Mr. Jackson."

The lieutenant turned his head toward the ridge, swearing softly. Forty or more dismounted Indians were strung along the summit.

"We'll take cover in that little creek depression—what cover there is. Have the horses drawn back into the ravine!" Bullets were already whistling overhead, pinging and skipping into the rocks.

For an hour a sort of stalemated contest of marksmanship ensued, the troopers pinned down among the jagged rocks where Clear Creek ran, the Arapahoes holding the ridgetop. The advantage, as Westcott was quick to concede, lay with the Indians. They had rifles, weapons of longer range and sharper accuracy than his cavalry carbines. Also, the hostiles were almost invisible, being of the same color as the coppery rocks where they lay. Only an occasional puff of white smoke from their rifles marked their presence as targets.

Meanwhile the day was draining away, and C Troop was no closer to Fort Wicked. At the last count, four troopers were dead, fourteen wounded.

He crawled over to where Lieutenant Jackson and Sergeant Connors were bellied down behind a log. "They can keep us here all day," he said without preliminaries. "We can't charge that ridge, we can't cross the creek—without chancing a disaster. If we go back into the ravine they'll have us dead for rights —as Connors said, they could rock us to death."

The lieutenant rubbed a thumb along his dry lips. "I suppose we just hold out till dark, then, sir?"

"Fort Wicked can't wait that long. I'm going to try another parley with Wolf Moccasin, try talking some sense into the old savage's head. Right now, I'm prepared to offer him that missionary on a silver platter—if he'll let us through to Fort Wicked."

Connors spoke up somberly: "You figger they've left anything at Fort Wicked, includin' the missionary?"

Westcott's jaw tightened. He did not reply.

"I'll volunteer to go talk with the old bastard," Jackson said. "If they're not beyond recognizing a flag of truce."

"They're too proud not to," Westcott replied. "But you're now in command of the troop, Mr. Jackson. If anything happens to me, if I don't return by nightfall, it'll be up to you to break out of here in the dark."

Using a muslin towel fastened to a stick as a truce flag. Westcott started down the trail on foot, waving the white cloth from side to side. Except for the service revolver in his holster, he was unarmed. All firing had ceased, and there was no sign of an Indian anywhere—on the ridgetop or in the aspen thicket. Lingering smudges of smoke from grass clumps spun before the wind, the air heavy with a smell of ashes, the earth burned black on either side.

As he came to the ford, he saw the body of the dead trooper where it had been dragged ashore and scalped. Without hesitation, he walked on into the shallows, waving the truce flag. He was halfway across when he saw two Arapahoes rise from the brush. They were holding rifles aimed directly at him. One of them was Red Willow, his face freshly painted for battle.

"I come in peace," Westcott said, making the sign by clasping his hands in front of his body. "I come to talk with Wolf Moccasin." He stopped walking, bracing himself against the flow of the creek, the water lapping over into his boots. He repeated the statement, and then Red Willow lowered his rifle, beckoning him to come forward. The other brave stood aside, still keeping his weapon at ready.

When he stepped ashore, pulling against the tug of deep sand, he saw other warriors scattered among rocks and brush, all watching him alertly. Far down the draw were the sunlit tops of tepees against dark pines.

He kept pace behind Red Willow until they reached a tepee marked with a wolf's head and a moccasin. An ancient bearskin hung over the entrance. After a minute, the bearskin moved, and Wolf Moccasin appeared. He was not wearing his war bonnet, nor was he painted. He was dressed simply in a black and white calico shirt, black cloth leggings, and moccasins embroidered with beads and porcupine quills.

Westcott considered the unwarlike costume a good sign; he

made the peace gesture, but Wolf Moccasin did not return it. Instead the chief motioned toward a skin mat before his small outdoor fire, indicating that Westcott should sit there.

While Wolf Moccasin was settling himself on another mat across the fire, Westcott removed his boots and drained the water from them. At the same time he studied his surroundings. Squaws were tending cooking pots down the arc of tepees; two children were peering out at him from the flap of a nearby lodge. From somewhere far down the circle came the keening cry of a mourning squaw.

"I hear the wailing of squaws in your village," Westcott said. "Soon they will set fire to the dead warriors' tepees and slay their horses after the old customs of Wolf Moccasin's people. Soon these widows will gash themselves with knives and cut off their hair. It is a bad day in Wolf Moccasin's village."

Wolf Moccasin nodded solemnly, as he poked at the small fire.

"Some brave warriors have died this day," Westcott continued. "Some brave soldiers have died this day. I have lost four who were like brothers to this soldier-chief. Others are wounded." He drew out his tobacco pouch and placed it near the fire so that it was within easy reach of the chief. Wolf Moccasin glanced away from it. He was not yet ready to accept a peace offering.

"If the chiefs—you and I," Westcott said, "if we can not make peace, our best young men will die before the sun goes over."

"Nahani," Wolf Moccasin replied hoarsely. "Soldier-chief take bluecoats away—back north. No one die."

"I must go on with my soldiers to Fort Wicked. The great soldier-chief has ordered me to march there and keep the peace."

Wolf Moccasin appeared to be pondering Westcott's words, searching the meaning in them. Partly in English, partly in Arapaho, he replied that the bluecoat pony soldiers must not go to Fort Wicked until the missionary, Metcalfe, was surrendered to the Arapahoes. The tribal council, the medicine men, had so decreed. The excrement-eating dog, Metcalfe, had desecrated the sacred lodge and had violated the Earth Mother. He must die, it was so decreed. And if Red Willow's brother died, one of the walking soldiers also must be surrendered to the Arapahoes.

The old chief's harangue was a long one, and Westcott was not certain he understood all of it. But at least one thing was clear. They did not have Metcalfe, yet.

"Where is Metcalfe?" he asked pointedly.

"In trading place of Agent Carlin. Walking soldiers there. Warriors burn what is wood, but inside is like white man's fort. Will not burn." As the chief spoke, haltingly, Westcott visualized the old trading post with its sign, *FORT WICKED*, rocking in the wind, the rotted sand-filled gunny sacks packed around logs and stones, the redoubt shape of it, the crude bastions, flanks, and roof parapet. The frame kitchen and bedrooms would have burned, but the original structure was solid, and a few armed men might stand off a siege for a long time.

"Soon they go mad for water," Wolf Moccasin said.

That is the vulnerable point, Westcott thought. *Water. And if she is still alive, Julie must be in there. Julie.* He could almost hear her voice pleading, *I want to go with you,* her violet eyes filling with tears. And he had sworn to her, *I promise you I'll be back.*

He fought the anger rising in him, and resumed his patient pleading, swearing on his honor to Wolf Moccasin that Metcalfe would be dealt with severely. But the chief was adamant, and Westcott at last knew that no matter what he promised, his words would have no meaning to the Arapahoes. They wanted Metcalfe, and they knew that eventually they would have him —if the cavalry troop could be kept away from Fort Wicked.

When he was certain that further talk was useless, Westcott arose, and using the few Arapaho phrases he knew began a formal speech of parting. He was cut off suddenly in mid-sentence by the chief: "Soldier-chief Westcott stay here."

Westcott picked up the truce flag. "Soldier-chief come here in peace," he said. "Now go in peace."

On either side of him were the warriors who had brought him to Wolf Moccasin's tepee—Red Willow and the other one, both painted for war. When Westcott's hand went down for his revolver, something struck him from behind, at the base of his neck.

He plunged forward across the fire, feeling the sudden heat of it in his belly, smelling the scorch of burning kersey. Hands were all over him at once, dragging and rolling him as he struggled. When the action stopped, he lay on his side, his wrists and ankles bound tightly with rawhide. A knotted rope bit into his legs above each knee.

Red Willow stood looking down at him, his face cruel under its smears of red and ochre.

Westcott rocked his head back, searching for the chief, pain darting out of the numbness of his bruised neck. Wolf Moccasin had disappeared, probably back into his tepee.

A little knot of braves had formed around him. One of them grunted, then two came forward and lifted his bound ankles. They began dragging him along the pinestraw-littered earth before the tepees, and as they passed each opening, eyes watched him—squaws' eyes in which timidity and awe were mingled, but no pity. He struggled to keep his head from the ground to avoid stones, but his blouse and shirt bunched at his shoulders and his naked back was bruised raw by the time they halted. He was in front of a closed tepee. Inside was the wailing squaw he had heard below.

When the Indians dragged him inside, she stopped her toneless lament. One of the warriors spoke sharply to her in Arapaho, then they all went out, closing the flap.

Westcott's nostrils filled with the gamy scent of old skins and blankets, of ancient smoke and grease. Where his body was not numbed, it ached, and he was grateful for the semidarkness.

A momentary wave of lassitude was engulfing him when the flap was flung open again, and five or six squaws peered inside, entering one by one. They left the closure lifted, afternoon sunlight slanting in upon them. He looked at their faces, hoping to recognize one he might have known at the agency, but he had seen none of these women at the agency. They were the squaws of the renegade Greasy Face warriors, friends of Yaneka Snell. These were the women he had found that summer day in the south village wearing dresses from the stolen trousseau of Anna Llewellyn.

One of them spat in his face and said something in Arapaho that was like a malediction. His mind translating dully, he realized she had mocked his rank and his red hair: "Captain Fire Hair."

Another one leaned close to him, holding her hands over his red hair as if to warm them, then without warning jerked a lock of it from his head. His scalp burned cruelly, but he made no outcry. If he showed pain or fear, he knew, they would only intensify their small tortures.

He lay quietly, watching them with pretended indifference, and when another one bent to take a similar prize, using a knife, he did not flinch against the metal or the spurt of warm blood—somehow enduring repetition of this ritualistic cruelty, with their little cries of exultation, until all had taken tufts of his hair.

From outside the tepee then, came a guttural command, and a shadow filled the tepee opening. One of the braves stood there, rifle cradled loosely in one arm. The squaws filed out. Again the skin closure fell and blocked the sunlight.

Westcott breathed deeply, grateful once more for the semi-darkness. Somewhere over on the far side of the tepee, the mourning squaw resumed her plaintive weeping, softly, in a singsong of grief.

Pain swept over him in a flood, nausea contracting his stomach. He stared up through the tepee's smokehole at the far circle of sky, then lay over on one side retching. Afterward, he felt an unconquerable desire to rest and sleep.

15

AS DUSK FELL OVER THE LODGES OF THE ARAPAHOES, A pinto pony bearing two riders turned into the camp from the Fort Wicked trail. The reinsman was John-day, wearing a broad white sombrero; the rider behind the saddle was Julie. At first glance in that hazy twilight, no one would have recognized her as a white girl, costumed as she was in a dark brown blanket skirt, with a second blanket covering her head and shoulders.

John-day guided the pinto up past Wolf Moccasin's tepee and along the arc of the camp to a small smoke-stained lodge. He dismounted, securing the pony to a pine tree, making no move to assist the girl, but turning directly toward the tepee and lifting the entrance flap.

"Wakeesa," he called softly, and when a voice answered out of the darkened lodge, he spoke rapidly in Arapaho.

Julie slid off the pinto's sweated rump, almost losing her blanket skirt which was fastened clumsily around her hips with bent pieces of wire. Her face was marked with briar scratches, her hair clotted with dried mud. In her eyes was a heaviness of fear and fatigue and grief that even her youth could not defy.

She looked around helplessly at her strange surroundings, dimly aware of a biting chill in the air and the sharp winy smell of pines. Someone called her name in a whisper, and she saw Wakeesa in the tepee entrance—Wakeesa, a friend, the sister of John-day's dead mother.

Repressing a sob of relief, Julie stumbled toward the Indian woman, letting her head rest for a moment on Wakeesa's breast before the squaw led her inside. A tiny smokeless fire burned in the center of the lodge.

John-day had seated himself on a willow-frame bed covered

with mats and buffalo skins. He pushed his white sombrero
back and smiled at the girl across the firelight. "Come sit," he
said cheerfully. "John-day's bed."

She went over and sat beside him, rubbing her hands together
to drive away numbness and cold.

Wakeesa hung a cooking pot over a forked stick, heaping red
coals beneath it. She began talking rapidly to John-day in Arapaho. Her voice and gestures revealed her agitation, and Julie
could tell from the way John-day leaned forward, the way his
leg muscles tightened under his jean trousers, that he was excited by what his aunt was telling him.

After a minute or so, he stood up, his handsome olive-
skinned face hard and determined. He drew his revolver from
its holster—an old Colt single action that had been a gift from
Brad Carlin—and held it close to the fire, checking the load. He
thrust it back in its holster, and then without a word to
Wakeesa or Julie, walked out of the tepee, dropping the skin
closure behind him.

Julie sat with her knees right together, listening to John-day's
footsteps fading as he walked away into the night. She looked at
Wakeesa, who glanced up and began moving her hands in fluid
expressive gestures until Julie understood that she was to lie
down and rest until food was ready.

With an involuntary sigh, the girl lifted her legs upon the
willow-frame bed, pulling her dangling blanket skirt over them,
her head dropping back among the old buffalo skins. All around
her was the strong male scent of John-day, and she stirred uneasily. She was in John-day's bed, the one Wakeesa kept for him
because he was the son of her dead sister. Her head swirled with
dizziness, a flow of recent memories crowding in upon her. She
ran one hand down below her throat, momentarily comforted
by the locket that lay there, knowing that Ben Westcott's picture was there, but memories raced again and she struggled
against panic, a nightmare from which she could not awake.

Was it yesterday or day before yesterday, or the day before
that? Time had collapsed upon itself in a kaleidoscope of horror
and death. She remembered only that the terror had begun on a
peaceful morning, a beautiful morning. She had been thinking
of Captain Ben Westcott that morning, looking more than once
into the locket she wore, studying his portrait, knowing he was

coming back as he had promised, sure that she had never been so happy before in her life.

Brad also had been unusually cheerful that morning, making his familiar old jokes. At breakfast he had said to Sergeant Kilfoyle that the Arapahoes had cooled off. "If they were going to show any force, they'd have done it before now," Brad said. "They've heard—God knows how they found out—that Ben Westcott is coming down from Yellowhorse with C Troop. If they intended to cut didoes, they wouldn't have waited this long."

"All the same, I don't trust 'em," was Kilfoyle's rejoinder. "I don't like the way they look at my men, as if they've taken a hate for soldiers they didn't have before."

"Well, that sun dancer got his head bashed in. And it *had* to be Red Willow's brother. But that'll blow over."

"Another thing," Kilfoyle went on, "the Greasy Faces won't leave without their rifles, and they're troublemakers."

"The Greasy Faces'll wait all right," Brad reassured him, "till the cavalry get here. Just keep a double guard on them confiscated rifles. So long as the bucks are not armed they can't do much damage." He pushed his chair back from the breakfast table. "Well, I reckon I better take old Metcalfe his coffee and bacon. He don't like to be kept locked up in the storeroom, but he sure enjoys his food."

Julie remembered now how Brad and Kilfoyle had gone out into the golden morning to start their daily rounds, still talking, the sergeant shaking his head dubiously. She was drying the breakfast dishes, thinking about Ben Westcott again and wondering what it would be like to be an Army wife, when she heard the first rifle fire.

It seemed to come from everywhere, all around the agency, the explosive echoes of fire, followed by shouts and shrill cries, and dogs barking like mad. Then from the infantry camp—the sudden desperate beating of a drum, the long roll, which she had never heard before yet knew from its urgency of rhythm that it was a call to danger.

She was standing at the kitchen door, the drying cloth in her hands, when she first saw Brad with Sergeant Kilfoyle and a little scattering of infantry soldiers moving almost furtively in and out of the willows along the creek. Individually they would

stop and aim and fire, then dart away, doing this over and over
again, all the while approaching the trading store. From closer
at hand, then, came a rattle of fire, almost a volley, with bullets
screaming and spanging against the wall of the kitchen. She
jumped back in alarm, and before she closed the door saw
twenty or more Indians on foot along the high ground beyond
the old commissary building. They were all armed, and coming
off the parade in short zig-zag dashes, dropping to the ground,
then rising and running forward again. She glanced back toward the creek. Kilfoyle and the soldiers were nearing the trading store, some following the beaten path, others in the dry
gully that ran down from the commissary. Brad was no longer
with them.

She closed the kitchen door, dropped the wooden bar in
place, and hurried to a window. But before she could push the
curtains back, her attention was distracted by a loud hammering noise. At first she thought it might be Metcalfe wanting to
know what was happening, but it was Brad banging on the front
door and calling her name.

When she let him in, he caught her close, his arms tightening
around her. "Thank God," he said. "Thank God, they didn't
come here first!" He barred the door, then hurried past the end
of the counter, reaching for his old shotgun, and went on into
the kitchen.

He told her nothing of what had happened, or what was
happening, only ordered her to stay in the trading room, and in
a few minutes, Sergeant Kilfoyle and seven of his men were
inside, Brad letting them through the kitchen door. Nobody
told her where the other nine soldiers were.

But as the day wore on and there were long periods of waiting while nothing happened, she learned from the men's talk
that two guards at headquarters had been killed instantly. The
other missing seven had been on mounted duty around the
agency, and were presumed to be dead or captured. The Indians
who had slain the guards had been armed with infantry rifles,
Kilfoyle said. They had broken into the storeroom where ammunition was kept.

"I reckon," Brad said, "that's why they didn't come here first
—for Metcalfe. They needed ammunition."

Julie could recall very clearly the incidents of that first day, how two of the men made a dash outside for a ladder, how they had hauled it inside, braced its legs against the counter, and run it out through a ceiling trap to the roof parapet. After Sergeant Kilfoyle took his best marksman up there, they were able to drive the besiegers all the way back to the edge of the parade ground.

During the afternoon, two incidents occurred out on the main trail. First, when the daily stagecoach came rolling in from the east, a party of Indians rushed to intercept it, firing before they were well in range, so the driver was able to turn the vehicle and apparently escape. Later, two passing wagons were attacked, one driver was shot dead, the other cut his horses loose and fled.

Sergeant Kilfoyle was hopeful that those who had escaped would spread the alarm and rouse the countryside, but Brad was less optimistic. "They'll warn other travelers back, yeah, but the cattle ranchers are too far scattered out," he said. "Be a day or two at best before they could help us, and Westcott should be here by then."

Later during the day, the men rolled three empty barrels into the trading room, lining them up along the counter, and Julie helped carry water from the kitchen pump. After they filled the barrels, Brad told her she should bring bedding, clothing, and whatever keepsakes she might treasure, from her room behind the kitchen. "This old trading room ought to stand, but I don't know what's to stop 'em burning the kitchen and bedrooms."

He removed the curtains over the opening between the store and the kitchen, and stacked bags of grain and flour and meal, three deep and solid, into the space, soaking them with water.

Just before dusk, Obadiah Metcalfe was released from the storage room. "Take a look outside, Metcalfe," Brad said bitterly, adding: "You're free to go now if you want."

Metcalfe's bony shoulders drooped under his torn black coat. He shuffled across the room, hovering like a scarecrow behind a soldier at one of the windows. He blinked out at the shadowy landscape. "Why do they do this?" His voice was hoarse, almost a croak. "What do they want?"

"They want you, Metcalfe," Brad replied. "If we let them have you, they'd go away."

Metcalfe made no answer, moving back to the wall and

squatting on his haunches, his gaunt face bent forward. Rifle fire banged from the parade ground, and the soldier at the window squeezed his trigger, the close explosion bringing an involuntary cry from the missionary. The soldier looked around, addressing no one, his voice derisive: "If he was half a man he'd volunteer to go out there and give hisself up. Spare that girl, Miss Julie, all this—" He cut his words off and turned back to the window.

That night, as Brad had feared, the Indians set fire to the kitchen and bedrooms.

It was from that time, from the moment she saw the first blaze shooting up on the farther roof that Julie's memory of events was blurred. She remembered how they had climbed the ladder to the roof parapet, all except Brad who stayed below to pour water upon the grain sacks blocking the rear door. Sergeant Kilfoyle ordered her to lie down on the south side away from the blaze, and Metcalfe was somewhere near her, sniffling and mumbling to himself.

The fire seemed to last forever, vicious tongues of flame leaping over the north parapet, and the soldiers were shooting almost continuously. When at last the heat died away, frosty air bit through her scorched dress, and she was shivering when she went back down the ladder. She remembered Brad's face as he helped her down, pale and sick-looking. He stopped his coughing long enough to tell her to lie flat on the bedding at the rear; there was less smoke along the floor, he said.

She must have slept; she remembered nothing else of that night. A burst of rifle fire brought her awake with a loud cry of fright. Sergeant Kilfoyle, at one of the windows, turned his grimy face toward her, smiling without humor. It was morning.

Brad was at another window, staring out toward the parade ground. "You notice anything different out there, Sergeant?" His voice was tired. "They've dismantled the tepees, every last one."

Kilfoyle peered out through the morning haze. "Damn me, if they haven't! Why, do you suppose?"

"Moving somewhere, leaving the agency."

Obadiah Metcalfe was crouched at the fireplace, warming his hands over the small fire on the hearth, and Julie wondered if she looked as bedraggled as he did. She brushed her tangled hair back over her ears, smoothed her wrinkled dress, and decided she looked presentable enough to start coffee boiling for the soldiers' breakfast.

"Look across there!" Kilfoyle cried. "I'd swear it's a white man!"

Brad turned back to the window. "It sure as hell is. Bearded." He took the raised field glass from the sergeant's hand. "It's Yankee Snell!"

Julie stopped in the middle of the room, cold fear gripping her heart. Snell! If Brad had said it was the Devil out there she knew she would not have been more frightened. She forced herself toward the window.

And there he was, at the edge of the parade, seated on a huge bay, his long beard a streak of black across his front. He held the horse immobile, as if both rider and animal were under a hypnotic spell.

Along the frost-browned grass of the slope were little moving specks of white, chickens freed from the barnlot by the night fires. One of the white spots exploded in a flurry of feathers; a rifle shot echoed, and she saw that Snell had moved, was holding his rifle up. He shot another, then another of the chickens, and she could hear his mirthless laughter echoing faintly down the slope.

"What's the damn fool doing that for?" Kilfoyle asked, bewildered.

"Because he's Snell, Yankee Snell." Brad's voice was bitter. He balanced his rifle on the window ledge and fired, but the range was too great, and Snell took cover casually behind some scrub trees.

"Who's he, you want to kill him? A squaw man?"

"Married into the tribe, yeah, he did that. He's a black-hearted murderer, Sergeant."

Another horse appeared from behind a lone poplar beyond Snell, the rider jerking awkwardly in the saddle, a man in Army blues. Kilfoyle had his glass up. "God help us," he cried, "it's Private Snowden. Trussed up and tied in the saddle!"

A soldier at one of the other windows echoed his words: "That's Snowden out there, Sergeant!"

Snell had taken the rope halter off Snowden's horse and was beginning to angle down the slope, keeping the helpless soldier between him and the trading store. Once Brad bent to sight along his rifle, but held his fire.

At the dry ditch below the commissary building, Snell halted, his beard thrusting out as he shouted: "Carlin! You in there, Carlin?"

"What you want, Yankee?"

Snell's laughter boomed in reply. "You had enough, Carlin? You want this soldier boy back alive? You want these Indians off your back?"

"Move away from the soldier, Yankee, and you'll get what's owing you."

Again Snell laughed. On tiptoes behind Brad, Julie could see nothing of the man but his beard, shaking as he laughed. Brad had his rifle up; he swore under his breath and eased the barrel down again.

"I want to talk to that gal of your'n, Carlin. She's in there."

"Go to hell!" Brad shouted.

"Ask her where the money is, Carlin. The greenbacks. You're a trader, Carlin—tell me where the greenbacks are and I'll stop all this shootin'." Brad wheeled, his face twisting in astonishment. "Julie—"

"I'll tell," she whispered. "The money's evil, Brad. I'll tell."

"*What* money, girl?"

"The payroll money he took from the wagon train. I hid it in the cellar, that old commissary cellar! Please God, tell him, Brad, so he'll go away."

Brad rubbed his fingers across the sprouting beard on his chin, his tired, smoke-reddened eyes disbelieving.

"Mr. Snell! Mr. Snell! Praise God, I am delivered!" It was Metcalfe's voice, desperate, a hoarse croak that could not have carried half way to the bearded man waiting at the ditch.

"Shut up, Metcalfe." Brad's hand fell on Julie's shoulder, his fingers tightening. "We'll tell him nothing, girl. He'd only take the money and run. That wouldn't change anything."

He turned back to the window. "Get out of here, Yankee, I warn you, get out or I'll kill you with less mercy than you killed Maude!" He fired across the front of the horses, the scream of the bullet setting the bay to dancing . . .

* * *

. . . Julie remembered now how Snell had cursed, how he had fought his horse, and pulled back up the slope, keeping the trussed soldier between him and the trading post until he was under the big balsam poplar, almost out of range. She remembered the outraged cry of Sergeant Kilfoyle: "They're torturing Snowden, sir! Bound him to that tree and burning him! And that bearded man just setting there on his horse doing nothing to stop it."

. . . She remembered the eerie piercing screams of the tortured soldier, the muttering of Kilfoyle, and her own voice, strange to her ears: "Tell him where the greenbacks are, Brad. So he'll stop. Tell him!"

"No, money wouldn't stop that, not money."

Kilfoyle's rifle butt banged on the floor. "I can't stand no more of that, Mr. Carlin. I'm taking one of my men down to that ditch, in range. If we can't drive 'em away from that tree, we can at least stop Snowden's misery."

"Wait." Brad blocked Kilfoyle's movement toward the front door. "Wait a minute, Kilfoyle. Your post is here, holding out till Captain Westcott comes. This is my burden." He shoved the wooden bar back from the door, the bell jangling as he flung it open. "I've got an old score to settle with that black-bearded devil."

Julie rushed after him, but the door slammed in her face. She ran back to the window, saw him come into view as he circled the building and passed the blackened ruins of the kitchen and the bedrooms. He was bent over, moving at a fast jog-trot, his rifle balanced in one hand. He went on to the ditch, seemed to hesitate a moment, then climbed out on the far side, still moving up the hill in that steady crouching jog-trot.

. . . She remembered how small he looked out there against the brown sweep of earth, all alone. Then suddenly he was down on one knee, firing, and she remembered the Indians scattering away from the poplar tree, the soldier hanging there by his ropes. Snell's horse reared, its shrill whinny cutting the cold air. And then Brad went down, as if he'd been crushed to earth by some invisible force. She could bear no more, choking off the scream in her dry throat, driven by a compulsion she could not resist to save Brad somehow by telling Snell where the greenbacks were hidden, impelled to run, run, run, through the unbarred door and across the ashes of the fire, running toward the ditch, seeing Brad's crumpled figure against the earth, running, running, and falling into the ditch.

As she lay gasping, her heart thumping, pressed against the dry clay of the ditch slant, she heard Kilfoyle's shouts—urgent, demanding—then footsteps behind her and a horse's hoofs beating the grass. She could run no more, and waited, waited for the footsteps behind her. But they did not slow or falter, became instead a shadow leaping past, the footsteps pounding again beyond her, and when she raised her head she saw it was Obadiah Metcalfe, already on the slope, straining, running in his queer stalking gait, his torn coat flapping, his voice a hoarse croak: "Mr. Snell! Mr. Snell! Providence! Providence! You have delivered me, Mr. Snell! Praise the Lord!"

Her hair had fallen over her eyes, and she pushed it away, and even now could feel the cold horror she had felt then—the sweeping wave of Indians descending upon Metcalfe, savage hatred in their faces, and the agonized voice of the missionary: "Mr. Snell, in God's name—"

And then John-day had come, galloping on his pinto, lifting her easily behind his saddle, the pony moving away in a fluid motion, like wind.

Suddenly they were in the willows with yellow-brown leaves falling like rain, and John-day swung her down roughly, pushing her away from the pony. "Stay here. Hide. John-day come back." Before she could speak, he was gone, the brim of his sombrero flapping, the pinto swinging in and out of the willows.

She hunkered down on the sand, stopping her ears against that high unearthly demon's cry from the slope, holding her palms steady until they began to tremble. When she dropped them, she heard a horse coming off the slope, splashing in the stream. Instinctively she scurried deeper into the willows, crawling like some hunted animal over the sand, briars scratching at her face and hands, on into the carpet of rustling leaves, burrowing until she felt mud oozing between her fingers.

A voice was calling John-day's name. Snell's voice, freezing her motionless. He repeated his calling, swore angrily, then rode away, down toward the soldiers' empty quarters.

. . . She remembered how she was trembling uncontrollably when John-day returned, almost without a sound he had appeared, leading the pinto. He gave her two brown blankets and some pieces of wire. "Change to Indian girl," he said. "Take off white woman dress. Make blanket dress." He turned his back, waiting, and when she had changed, awkwardly—her fingers were numb and useless as if frozen—he motioned her to mount and then he led the pony out.

He was alert, his muscles taut, listening and watching, until they crossed the creek and reached the deserted trail to the north. He grunted with satisfaction. "Arapaho all go see Metcalfe die."

She had not asked him where Snell was, remembering only that she had locked her arms around John-day's waist as the pinto gathered speed, thinking of Brad left back there crumpled on the slope. She had prayed silently to God that Brad not be dead, and thanked Him for John-day, who had saved her like a knightly brother.

* * *

. . . She remembered it all, the past sweeping by her like a rushing river. And now the present crowded in again—the smell of pinewood smoke and boiling meat, the male scent in the old buffalo robes—and she sat up in the strange bed, praying that when she opened her eyes she would know the terror had been only a dream.

But she was still inside the tepee, and Wakeesa was bent over the cooking pot, spooning soup into a wooden bowl.

What would happen to her now? She remembered the last hour of the ride, how after they sighted the tepee smokes, John-day had begun to boast. He would make her his squaw woman now, he said. At first she joked with him, scratching her fingers down his back, but he only bragged the more—of his bravery, his strength, and his cunning. Tonight he would make her his woman, he had said, and there was no bantering in his tone . . .

Wakeesa was smiling at her across the fire. She brought the soup bowl over to the bed, placing it in Julie's lap. Steam arose, aromatic and tantalizing, but she could not eat.

The squaw drew away, watching the girl, making the sign for eating, puzzled because Julie did not do so. "Eat," she said in English.

Julie shook her head, forcing a smile.

"You fear?" Wakeesa asked.

The girl nodded shame-facedly, almost with a child's expression of embarrassment. "I fear John-day," she said.

Comprehension came quickly to Wakeesa's face. She made a gesture that a sheltered white woman would have considered extremely lewd, laughing in the soft repressed way of a squaw. "Is not bad thing," Wakeesa said. "Is good, you no make fuss."

"No, no." Julie shook her head in desperation. "Not want to be John-day's squaw."

Wakeesa shrugged, turned her back and began searching for something in the shadows around her bed. She returned with a long coil of thin rope. Julie shrank back, her first thought that Wakeesa intended to tie her, but the woman spoke soothingly in Arapaho, drawing open the twisted blanket Julie wore for a skirt, unbending the crude wire fastenings, and removing it entirely.

She showed Julie how to wrap the rope closely around her body, beginning at the waist, spiraling it down over her thighs —all the while reminiscing in mixed English and Arapaho of how when she was a young girl she had so protected herself at times by winding a lariat from her waist to her ankles.

Her fingertips touched the lower part of Julie's thigh. "So far, enough. John-day understand."

After Julie had secured the rope, Wakeesa brought a bone needle and some thin strips of rawhide, and began working over the old brown blanket, fastening it around the girl's hips, and sewing it together at the folds.

When she had finished she poured the cold soup from the bowl back into the pot, and spooned up a hot portion. "Eat now," she said.

Julie was eating soup when she heard John-day's footsteps returning. She leaned forward, the tight spiral of rope under her skirt binding against her thighs. Her eyes were fixed on the tepee closure, and when John-day lifted the skin, night air flowed in sharp and clean as ice. John-day was standing there, his white sombrero cocked at an angle, smiling triumphantly at her.

*   *   *

Squatting before the fire, John-day finished the soup in the pot and began sucking marrow from a bone. He spoke occasion-

ally to Wakeesa in Arapaho, the squaw replying in short sub-
dued phrases. The fire died gradually, darkness and cold deepening simultaneously inside the tepee.

Julie sat upright on the low bed, scarcely moving or breathing, conscious of the protecting rope around her. She began
shivering, but did not want to draw John-day's attention, and so
was afraid to lie down and cover herself with the robes.

After a while, Wakeesa sighed, said something softly in Arapaho and padded over to her bed. Julie could hear her rolling
about in the skins for a minute, then she was quiet.

John-day was moving somewhere beyond the red coals of the
fire, his hands working at his saddlebag. A strong scent of
sweetgrass filled the air, and Julie knew he was greasing his
hair.

She could feel his presence before she heard him, his hands
gentle on her face, the odor of sweetgrass strong in her nostrils.
"Hisa," he whispered, caressing her with his cheek as she had
taught him long ago, a gesture of brother and sister love, she
had told him.

"Julie shake like leaf in cold wind," he said softly. "John-day
make warm, warm."

Her resistance was not equal to the pressure of his arms, and
she lay back on the matting, letting him arrange the skins and
robe over her, grateful for the warmth. He lay beside her for a
minute, his hands moving awkwardly until they found the binding rope around her thighs.

She felt the sudden suspiration of his warm breath against her
ear, then he moved away from her. "So," he said, then muttered
to himself, wounded and angry. He slid off the bed and stalked
over to the coals, heaping on wood. When he sat cross-legged,
she could see his scowling profile like a black cardboard cutout
against the yellow firelight.

"John-day is brother," the girl said quietly. "Julie is sister.
But not squaw for John-day."

He replied without looking at her: "John-day wait. Julie be
squaw soon."

"No," she said. "John-day take Julie to one of soldier forts."

She saw the firm shake of his head. "John-day wait. Julie no
place for sleep, eat. No father no more. No mother. John-day
wait. Julie be squaw soon."

"For money you will take me to one of the soldier forts?"

"Money? Where Julie get money now."

She whispered, not wanting Wakeesa to hear: "I gave you money twice. There is much more where that came from, enough greenbacks to fill that old saddlebag."

He rose and came over to the bed, looking down at her. "Where this money?"

"You take me to soldier fort, I tell you where money is."

"Why Julie go soldier fort?"

She hesitated a moment. "Captain Westcott will find me if I am in one of the forts."

His face was close to hers. She could see the sheen of his greased hair, and a strange exultance in his eyes that was also in his voice as he replied: "Soldier-chief Westcott not find Julie. Soldier-chief prisoner. Is in the lodges. He die soon."

As he spoke, all the warmth of the protecting robes seemed to flow away from her, leaving a dull aching under this final blow, the nightmare turning inward upon itself. She wanted desperately to weep, but she was beyond weeping now.

His hand came down roughly against her throat, his fingers wrapping around the frail chain of her locket. He tugged at it, snapped it loose. She made no outcry of pain, only lay quietly looking up at him. He turned toward the fire, thrusting the locket into his pocket. "Where is money?" he demanded loudly.

She sat up, gathering the robes around her. "Free Captain Westcott," she replied, "and I'll tell you where."

"Tell me now," he said.

She shook her head, staring back at him. He bent down and began stirring the fire with a stick. Outside, a horse was moving closer, the hoofbeats slow and heavy on the pine needles. The horse halted, a voice called out something in the night.

John-day raised his head, his eyes darting back to her in alarm. The hoofbeats began again, the horse snuffling as it halted outside the tepee. A rifle butt rattled against a saddle.

John-day had raised his boot, moving toward the fire as if to scatter the burning wood, then the tepee closure flung aside. A rifle barrel glinted, and Yaneka Snell entered.

For a moment the bearded man stood there, his enormous eyes blinking against the unfamiliar light, holding the rifle steady on the boy. His mouth worked under his black beard, his eyes shifting to the bed where Wakeesa lay, then back to Julie. "Homelike," he sneered. "You got her bedded down proper, ain't you, boy?"

"John-day's squaw. No other man touch now."

"I only married into this tribe," Snell drawled. "Didn't take to their ways." He moved closer to the fire. "But bein's you my blood boy, I'll buy her off you."

"Girl not for sale."

Snell steadied the rifle muzzle only a few feet from John-day's belly. "If you was anybody else, boy, I'd kill you with my bare hands, you causin' me all this trouble." He stepped sideways toward Julie. "Where's the greenbacks?"

She looked at him, hiding her fear with a mocking smile. "All burned," she said spitefully, "when the Arapahoes set fire to Brad's house."

"Julie lie!" John-day took a step toward her, holding himself back when Snell flung his rifle up. "Julie talk with crooked tongue to John-day!"

"She lies now," Snell said. "They had plenty time to get that money out." He frowned at the boy. "Where'd she tell you the greenbacks was hid?"

John-day shrugged. "No say where. Make promise. She lie."

Julie watched them furtively, saw the rival greeds building between them, and faint hope stirred within her. *Maybe if I tell them the hiding place they will both go away and then I can find Captain Westcott.*

"I lied," she confessed wearily. "I hid the greenbacks in the old commissary building, in the cellar under one of the shelves."

When she looked again at John-day's face she felt a sickness in her stomach. *He is doomed,* she thought. *They will both die now. I've doomed John-day with the evil of the stolen money.*

"We go look." John-day's voice was eager, his gestures almost patronizing as he turned toward Snell.

"She lied twice. Maybe she lies three times. She goes with us." Snell grinned at the boy. "Put her on your pony. Tie her on good."

It's all gone for nothing, she thought, *and so I am doomed, too.* She made only a token resistance, futility deadening her struggles, knowing that if she fought off John-day, then Snell and his cruelties would take the boy's place.

She let Wakeesa help unspiral the rope around her thighs, and when she was mounted on the pinto, John-day used the same rope to tie her legs securely. Snell circled the pony, checking the ties, his rifle cradled carelessly in one arm.

"Me ride with girl?" John-day asked.

Snell came around the front of the pinto facing the boy. "You stay here."

"No!" John-day was standing in the dancing beam of firelight from the tepee opening. His hand moved toward his revolver.

In that instant, Snell sprang out of the shadows, his rifle reversed, bringing the heavy butt down on the boy's head, sending the sombrero spinning, then crashing again upon the defenseless skull. John-day fell back, and without a sound dropped as if dead upon the ground.

16

WESTCOTT WAS CONSCIOUS FIRST OF COLD PENETRATING TO his bones, then of numbness in his arms and legs. From where he lay, he could see stars glittering through the tepee smokehole, and wondered how long he had slept. He heard a horse go thudding by slowly on the pine needles, then the only sound was a low moaning from the lamenting squaw back in the tepee's darkness.

He rolled over on his belly, working his legs and wrists against the rawhide thongs. The exertion warmed him slightly and eased the dullness out of his muscles, but he felt no lessening of pressure from the bonds.

For a while he lay still, listening, wondering if Lieutenant Jackson had started his move, waiting anxiously for carbine fire, the sound of galloping horses on the trail. He heard only the soughing of wind in the pines, an occasional crackling from the guard's fire outside the tepee, then a single horse running far away, and that was all.

Intermittently he worked at loosening the rawhide bindings, jackknifing his legs to force the rope at the knees. He managed to sit up, lean forward, and get his teeth into the rope. He was biting at the knot when he heard a new sound somewhere behind him, a sound like a long exhalation of breath. Cold air brushed his back, the clean smell of it driving away the permeating odor of dead smoke.

He raised his head, catching a faint scent of sweetgrass, and knew someone was behind him, felt then the steel of a knife against one of his palms.

Rawhide gave way before the blade; his hands were free. He brought them down to his sides, flexing his fingers. Someone touched him lightly and slipped a knife hilt into his right hand. In a moment he had severed the rope and the rawhide at his ankles. He came up in a crouch, barely hearing a hiss of breath that warned him to be silent. The grieving squaw still moaned in her bed of skins; the guard out front had not stirred.

Westcott forced his benumbed legs into motion, staggering a little, holding his hand out in the darkness. He was thankful when his rescuer took his wrist and led him the three or four steps to a long slit cut into the tepee covering. As soon as he was outside in the starlight, he could see John-day's youthful face, eager, expectant, under a dirty flap-brimmed sombrero.

With a single gesture, the half-breed cautioned him to move without sound, and they crept away from the tepee into a thickening stand of pines, then turned back, John-day moving faster, Westcott close behind, still fighting the stiffness in his legs.

They circled the rim of the camp, the boy half-trotting, then stopping in a black pool of shadow where two saddled horses were tied, and then moving on, leading their mounts through thick brush and over a rock-filled creek until they came to high grass that rattled as they pushed through it.

They faced the eastern butte, the rim haloed by a rising full moon. Beyond the grass was the main trail, and before they entered it the boy held up, listening, then led his horse out upon the dusty passage.

Westcott looked to the north, getting his bearings and estimating the Clear Creek ford to be a mile or more away, disappointed that John-day had brought him out on this side. He wondered if C Troop had broken out of the ravine while he still slept in the tepee.

John-day was securing the fastenings of his pack saddle; it was an old rawhide wooden frame with high pommel and cantle.

Keeping his voice low, Westcott asked: "Where are the soldiers, the bluecoat pony soldiers?"

The boy raised up from the side of his mount. He shrugged, shaking his head.

Westcott spoke again: "Can you take me back into the ravine, beyond the ford?"

Still holding his bridle, John-day moved around in front of the captain. He dug into his jeans pocket and brought out Julie's locket and broken chain, the metal glimmering faintly in starlight, holding them out in his open palm to Westcott.

Recognizing the locket immediately, Westcott's fingers closed upon it. He felt a sudden rush of blood pounding through his body, the hammering of his heart.

"Is she alive?"

"Is so. In great danger, Soldier-chief Westcott."

"Where?"

"On this trail. To agency, Fort Wicked. With one called Yankee."

"Snell!" He spoke the name as though it were something foul, moving toward his horse and swinging into the saddle. "Wait! Why with Snell?"

"Julie know where greenbacks hid. Yankee take Julie, show him money."

So that was the answer—he had almost guessed it before. *John-day's mysterious greenbacks, the missing payroll! And Julie was the key.* She would be safe only until the moment Snell was sure of the money.

When he released his reins, he used his spur unmercifully, and lunging away almost lost his seat. The saddle was an ancient Spanish type with short stirrup leathers, but he regained his balance and let his mount go to a gallop.

He kept the horse in full motion until the animal's hoarse breathing warned him to ease up. A few minutes later, John-day overtook him and they settled into a steady trot.

Preoccupied with his concern for Julie's safety, Westcott scarcely noticed that the moon was over the butte's rim, illuminating the basin with cold bluish light so that every rock and depression was marked by a black splash of shadow.

They had gone about two miles when John-day swung around abruptly, pointing forward, signaling with both hands to take cover. They dismounted quickly and led their horses down into the willow fringe of the creek. Three or four horses were coming fast from the south, the riders making little yelping cries of victory. As the Indians swept past in the bright moonlight Westcott could see the gleam of war paint on their faces. They were all young bucks, riding as if they were drunk.

Resuming the urgent journey, Westcott took the lead as they approached the last turn in the trail before Fort Wicked. The moon, lifting higher in the sky, lost its illusionary immenseness, by contrast seemed shrunken and wan.

Suddenly Fort Wicked lay ahead—the familiar smudge of its trees along the curving creek, the black squares of its old buildings. A huge fire burned on the parade ground, and even at this distance Westcott could see tiny leaping silhouettes of dancers ringing it. Several smaller cooking fires winked here and there, pale yellow under the blue moonlight.

His horse was almost spent, indrawn air whistling in its throat, flecks of froth blown back with each expulsion of breath, its legs rocking unsteadily. By the time he reached the first cluster of cottonwoods, John-day had overtaken him again. The boy pushed his sombrero back, lifting in his stirrups, peering off at the fire and the carousing dancers up on the parade.

"Where?" Westcott asked quietly. "Do you know—"

Turning slightly in his saddle so that Westcott could see his face clear in the moonlight, the boy answered: "Julie say in old commissary—may be so." He motioned Westcott to follow him, taking a rough path into the cottonwoods, weaving in and out along the creek. They crossed at a shallows, walking horses slowly to avoid splashing, then turned into the willows, keeping in a crisscross of shadows thrown by the leafless trees.

Now they were into the familiar path that led to Brad Carlin's trading store, and although he was prepared for it, expected it, Westcott felt an acute sensation of loss when he saw the charred ruins of the living quarters, recalling in a flash a hundred happy memories of Maude, Brad, and Julie. The solid old trading room still stood, but no light showed anywhere; it looked lifeless under the moonlight.

John-day reined his horse, beckoning Westcott to pull up beside him, pointing along the ditch across the slope. The dilapidated wooden shell of the commissary loomed against the sky, light and shadows playing upon its front from the dancers' fire on the parade.

Two horses were hitched beside the sagging entrance steps. One was John-day's pinto.

"There!" The boy's voice was so intent it shrilled. He was lifting his quirt when Westcott warned him: "Go slow. If we come clattering up there, we'll draw that crowd of crazy dancers down on us!"

It was agony for Westcott, keeping the horse to a walk, following along the ditch; he wanted to sink his spurs in the beaten animal's flank for one last dash, to rush in and— He needed a weapon, any weapon. Red Willow had taken his revolver back there in the tepee camp, and now he had not so much as a penknife.

He dropped back, riding close beside John-day's mount. "Let me have your revolver."

The boy's eyes shone brightly for a moment, wavering under the captain's insistent stare, but he shook his head doggedly, one hand falling to his holster. He pulled away without reply.

Westcott restrained his impulse to force the issue. The halfbreed trusted him only to a degree, he thought, but not beyond the point of surrendering the weapon to him. What was the boy's purpose, freeing him, furnishing a horse, leading him here? In the showdown, only one could win—Snell, John-day, or himself. The boy was cunning, he knew, had learned the value of money early, was hungry for its power. *Is he pitting me against Snell, hoping that each of us will cancel out the other?*

Ahead were the sagging steps of the commissary, the wide door hanging by one hinge. The pinto and the bay were haltered to a broken hitching rack, steam rising from their haunches. As Westcott came up, he reached out and touched the pinto's shoulder. It was warm and wet. Snell and Julie could not have been in the building more than a matter of minutes.

As he dismounted and secured his horse, he made a quick survey of the surroundings. The trading store was still dark, no sign of Brad Carlin or Sergeant Kilfoyle, or any of the infantrymen. In the opposite direction the dancers still leaped wildly around the big fire. Closer at hand, not more than fifty yards away, was a small cooking fire. He was surprised to see squaws there; he had assumed that all of them had gone with the lodges to the camp on Clear Creek.

He bent down and gathered a few stones, two or three as large as apples, loading his pockets. A man must use what weapons he can, he thought sardonically, and waited deliberately for John-day to make the next move.

"Julie say in cellar," the boy whispered.

"Give me the revolver," Westcott demanded, but the halfbreed made no reply, only hesitating a moment to adjust his sombrero, and then moving up the steps into the building. He walked like a cat, easing pressure whenever a board creaked.

Westcott followed closely. Streaks of moonlight splashed through the window shells. A disturbed night bird darted away with a ghostly flapping of wings.

As they neared the cellar steps they stooped low, almost crawling to the single post at the stairhead. Westcott braced himself and peered down the dimly lit slant of stairs.

Yellow lantern glow formed a circular spot of light a few yards beyond the bottom step. Along the outer rim of light against the wall was Julie—dressed in a blanket skirt like an Indian girl, her back to the stairs. She was taking bottles from a recessed shelf, one at a time, setting them carefully on the hard earthen floor.

A voice drawled up the stairs, harsh, impatient—Snell's voice: "You givin' me the fidgets. Hurry it up!"

Westcott had to move his head farther around the stair post to see the bearded man—back behind the lantern, slouched, favoring one leg, his rifle slung carelessly.

Julie began pulling wads of cotton from the shelf, dropping them at her feet. One hand went down in the recess, searching. She brought up a green packet of paper, holding it in the spray of lantern light. "Now, you believe me?"

Snell came forward, eyes squinting, his boots heavy on the dry earth. "Move away, over there." As he waved his rifle, the girl dropped the money back into the hollow shelf, and drew away, her face turned for a moment so that Westcott could see her clearly. There was no fear in her eyes, only resignation.

With a loud grunt of gratification, Snell reached for the pack of greenbacks. In his excitement, he leaned his rifle against the wall, and began digging into the hidden plunder. "By God, gal, you kept it for me, didn't you!" he cried exultantly. "Damn near all of it!"

Westcott moved so that his mouth was close to John-day's ear. "The lantern!" he whispered. The boy remained motionless, fascinated by the packs of greenbacks which Snell was pulling from the recessed shelf. "Shoot out the lantern!" Westcott repeated, his fingers tightening on the stone he held in his hand, the pressure reminding him of it, and he stood up, balancing carefully, aiming for the lantern, and hurled the stone. It missed the lantern by inches, bounding away down the cellar.

At the sound of impact, Snell spun around, his elbow knocking his rifle down with a scraping clatter. He swore, his bearded face turning toward the stairwell, his enormous eyes rolling.

John-day reacted quickly, springing up, one shoulder plowing into Westcott's hip, bringing his revolver into play. His first shot hit the lantern, exploding its glass shield. The cellar blotted into darkness, relieved only by little rectangles of moonlight marking the ventilator windows.

Four revolver shots rang out from below—*spang, spang, spang, spang,* hollow sounding. Westcott had flung himself away, out of range, but John-day lay flat on the floor. A sulphury smell of burned gunpowder floated heavy in the air.

"You hit?" Westcott asked softly.

"No." The boy crawled away from the stairhead, boards creaking beneath him.

"Westcott!" Snell's voice roared from the cellar.

The captain kept silent. From where he crouched he could look directly out one of the window shells to the nearest cooking fire; the squaws out there were moving about excitedly, perturbed by the sudden gunfire. "John-day." The half-breed's face came closer. "So?"

"We'll have to smoke him out."

"May be so."

"You crawl out that window, keep quiet about it. Bring faggots from that nearer fire. Make the squaws help. Plenty dry grass out there. Heap it around the ventilator windows. Make a lot of smoke—but don't set the building afire."

"Soldier-chief Westcott go make smoke," the boy replied sullenly. "John-day stay here."

"You know what your people would do to me if they caught me out there, unarmed." Westcott touched the boy's shoulder, still holding his voice to a strained whisper: "You don't want Julie hurt, do you?"

"No, Soldier-chief Westcott."

"Then go. It's our best chance to get her out of there alive. And give me your gun."

He could see the half-breed's mouth twist down, almost in a boyish pout. But John-day held on to the weapon, crawling away toward the shell of the window, making no more noise than a snake. His black shadow rose against the pale firelight, then vanished.

Westcott waited, his shoulder braced against the stairpost. A slight tremor in the wood warned him that Snell was on the steps. He drew a stone from his pocket, reached out, hurling it down at an angle. Snell's reply was a single shot, the bullet screaming out of the stairwell.

As he listened for the click of firing pin against an empty chamber, Westcott's leg muscles tightened. *He's fired five shots, his revolver should be empty—unless he's reloaded. But he has that rifle, too.*

"Damn you, Westcott! I know you're up there." Snell's voice was edged with frustration.

He'll lose his head, Westcott thought, *if I keep him guessing, wondering whether he's hit me. If I can draw him up here—*

"You want this girl to live, Westcott, speak up! I don't need her no more."

Westcott's fingers dug into his palms. Now he would have to chance it, chance rushing Snell in the dark, chance Julie escaping in the confusion—

He took one of the larger stones from his pocket and peered around the stairpost, listening, hoping to find Snell's position from the sound of his voice or his movements, rising slowly from his crouch, his muscles contracting for a quick rushing leap down the stairway.

"I'm counting to ten, Westcott, then I shoot her."

A moment later a little streak of orange flamed in one of the square ventilators; a flung sheaf of grass almost smothered it, then the fire burst into bright life, its sudden illumination startling Snell.

Westcott hesitated, measuring the distance to Snell's swinging shadow. He saw the big man's arm go up—he *had* reloaded his revolver—to fire blindly into the yellow-tinged smoke pouring through the ventilator.

Without warning Westcott leaped, hitting the center step of the stairway, letting his knees bend as he landed, using the upward spring to send him vaulting in a second leap toward Snell, then lunging as he hit the earthen floor.

Snell must have heard, or sensed Westcott's approach, for he was half-turned, one leg braced, shoulder raised, as he caught the impact of the captain's body, the stone in Westcott's hand crashing into his shoulder instead of his head. But Snell's revolver was shaken loose, spinning away over the dry-packed earth.

As Westcott spun off balance from his own forward rush, he heard Snell's outraged bellow of pain and tried to follow up his first attack with a quick punch to the belly, but missed as the big man staggered back.

More fires were burning in other ventilators now, smoke boiling inside, reflections of small fires relieving the gloom of the cellar. As he backed away from Westcott's off-balance punch, Snell's eyes rolled, searching frantically for his grounded revolver.

Westcott saw the weapon first, not more than a yard behind the bearded man's bootheels. He rushed in, feinted with his left, and rocked Snell back with a solid blow to the mouth. Blood spurted as Snell recoiled, and Westcott dived for the revolver. Before his left hand reached the weapon, Snell's boot came down, crushing his fingers. He came up fast, using his knees for leverage, but Snell was on him now, his huge, bearlike arms gripped around his neck, squeezing.

For a moment Westcott's right arm was free, and he found Snell's beard, wrapping his fingers into it, jerking until the neckhold was relaxed, and they both fell, rolling. They jammed into the wall, and in suspended motion, Westcott saw Julie for the first time since he had leaped into the cellar.

As flames flared up from a ventilator, he saw her clearly, crumpled like a lifeless doll, head bent forward, one arm outflung. In that flash of recognition all the fight drained out of him—he was sure that Snell had already shot her, deliberately, callously. The fight went out of him, and with it reason—fury replacing judgment. He wanted to kill now without reason, to destroy blindly.

He pulled away, reckless, ordering Snell to stand up, taunting him, daring him to get up and fight to the death. For a minute, Snell was bewildered, his bloodshot eyes darting to one of the blazing windows where the fire had gone out of control and was eating swiftly into the dry wood of the building. Thick smoke poured in, circling, lowering steadily toward the floor of the cellar.

Snell spat blood; it dribbled and mixed with the crimson streaks already staining his beard. He blinked nervously at the crackling fire above his head. "Let's get out of here, Westcott!"

"Stand up and fight!" Westcott said coldly. "I'm going to kill you anyway."

Ducking his head to avoid a swirl of smoke, Snell threw a quick glance at the scattered packs of greenbacks on the floor below the shelf. He began pushing himself up, using the wall at his back for support, and too late Westcott saw him go for the knife in his belt, at the same instant thrusting forward from the wall, his huge body hurtling toward Westcott. His red-smeared mouth yawped in a cry of rage, his knife up, obscured in the smoke.

At the moment of impact, Westcott sought the big man's wrist, but Snell twisted suddenly and the captain felt the sharp knife point rip his jacket. They broke away and began circling, facing each other like two alert and deadly wrestlers.

The fire was raging now, long tongues of it licking along the wooden flooring above their heads, smoke smarting their eyes.

It was then that a new sound broke above the crackle of the fire—a thudding of footfalls, and Westcott saw movement on the stairway through the screen of smoke behind Snell. His eyes swept back to his opponent, watching the knife, circling as the big man tried to move in, and then Snell saw the intruder.

For a moment Snell's eyes focused beyond Westcott, his forehead wrinkling, his bulging eyes straining. Suddenly he sprang, his booted kick sending Westcott sprawling backward. The captain rolled as he fell, coming to his feet in a choking cloud of smoke, expecting contact. But as the smoke cleared momentarily he saw Snell moving off toward the stairway. Someone else was beyond the big man—bent down over the strewn packs of greenbacks.

It was John-day, his face turned fearfully to the onrushing Snell. The boy arose, each hand gripping a pack of greenbacks, dodging when Snell slashed down at him. As the boy fell, Westcott saw Snell's rifle on the floor against the wall where it had dropped when John-day shot out the lantern.

In a matter of seconds, Westcott was across the floor, and had the rifle up as Snell turned on him. He swung the rifle as a club, the stock crashing into Snell's head, the big man collapsing as if he had been poleaxed.

Westcott sucked in his breath, choking, heat scorching at his back. He dropped to the floor, gulping for air, crawling toward the wall where Julie still lay crumpled and lifeless. He lifted her over his shoulder and stumbled back toward the steps. Behind him a burning board crashed, showering sparks; the sparks swept past him up the stairwell in a blasting draft.

He stepped over Snell's sprawled body, stooped to touch John-day's face. The cheek was split, and sticky to the touch. One of the boy's hands lay like a claw across his chest, the money held there soaked with blood.

Westcott staggered on up the steps, found his way across the smoke-filled upper structure to a window. When he lowered Julie to the sill, balancing her there, she moaned, a protesting moan, and her arms reached for him.

"Julie!" His voice was hoarse, almost breathless, but she knew him, her eyes fluttering open for a moment, and then her head fell against her shoulder. "You said you'd come back for me," she whispered, her mouth moving up against his chin.

He slid out the window, helping her down. In the moonlight her face looked shockingly pale and hollow.

"Julie, are you hurt?"

As she clung to him, he could feel her head shaking negatively, her forehead rubbing against his chest. "I just gave up," she said. "I couldn't stand any more, I thought you were dead, Ben Westcott, so I gave up."

* * *

The building is a pyre, Westcott thought, looking back over his shoulder at the leaping roaring flames. John-day was dead, but in dying he had saved two lives from Snell. Later, he would tell Julie that—not of the greed that had driven the boy.

Instinctively, he had taken cover in a dry ditch. Julie's arms were still about his neck. She began sobbing, uncontrollably.

As soon as they were out of the reflected heat, he stopped and peered over the edge of the ditch, seaching for the horses left at the east end of the building. They were gone. Someone had unhitched them.

Up on the parade ground were the Arapahoes, a long line of

them, watching the spectacle like children, the wild rites of their celebration temporarily forgotten, their dancing fire a feeble contrast to this grand conflagration.

Without horses, Westcott knew, he had to find cover quickly, before the fire died away. He turned toward the trading store; it was brilliantly lit by reflected glare, every detail sharp and clear. He saw the grain bags stacked in what had been the passageway to the burned kitchen.

"Julie?"

"Yes."

"Can you walk, run?"

"For you I can do anything."

"We must get into the old trading room. You go ahead of me, straight toward that stack of grain bags, as fast as you can move. I'll be right behind you."

He pushed her over the edge of the ditch, following, one hand on her arm, supporting her, urging her forward.

A moment later Sergeant Kilfoyle's voice rang out of the night: "Hold your fire! It's Captain Westcott!"

Westcott flung a protecting arm around Julie, moving on with her, then lifting her as she stumbled.

Around the corner of the building came Kilfoyle and two of his infantrymen, rifles flashing in the firelight. "This way, sir! Thank God, you've come!" The soldiers quickly covered the rear, and Westcott followed Kilfoyle around the east wall on to the familiar, battered old front door. The *FORT WICKED* sign still hung there, like a triumphant banner. As soon as his men were inside, Kilfoyle dropped the bar over the door, breathing hard.

"I don't think they even noticed, Sergeant," drawled a soldier at one of the windows. "Leastways none of the buggers made a move this way."

Westcott lowered Julie gently upon one of the mattresses on the floor. She sighed gratefully, her eyes closing when Westcott pulled a blanket over her.

"God help me," Kilfoyle cried, "it's Miss Julie! I thought she was Indian. And I thought the bastards had *her*."

Westcott raised his head. "She's going to be all right, Sergeant." He took a quick glance around the trading room. "Where's Brad Carlin?"

"Christ," Kilfoyle whispered. "Don't you know?"

"Sergeant!" The soldier at the window had one hand up, shading his eyes, peering out toward the parade. "Something peculiar going on out there."

Kilfoyle moved across to the adjoining window, Westcott close behind him. The commissary roof had collapsed, and the fire had turned a lurid orange. All along the slope the Indians were scattering. Then a line of horsemen appeared, like ghostly shadows beyond the fireglow.

"It's C Troop," Westcott said wearily. "They made it through."

17

JULIE WAS THINKING OF TIME, HOW MYSTERIOUS IT WAS, like the clouds, sometimes floating almost motionless, sometimes rolling so fast one might cry for it to stop. Motionless Time was always the best or the worst, yet even then it was deceptive, she knew, for Time never stopped. It was always taking her somewhere.

This morning she was mounted on the pinto that had been John-day's, a pony that had become a symbol, a remnant of memory, for there was nothing left of John-day, only the pinto. She remembered how the pony was meant to be a marriage offering, so long ago when time drifted like a dream.

Time had stopped for her only once—the night the commissary burned, but it had begun again, slowly, and then all at once the days rushed in a gallop, everything happening at once. New soldiers had come to Fort Wicked, and with them stern-faced government men, and there was talk, endless talk. Ben Westcott was in a dark mood much of the time; he said the government men were trying to punish the whole Arapaho people for the activities of a few hot-heads. "They don't understand," he said, "they've got to expect to take two steps backward for every three steps forward in these matters of pacifying the tribes."

At last a chubby, round-faced little man arrived. He was a Quaker missionary from Indian Territory, and Ben Westcott said he knew more about the Arapahoes than all the government men in Washington. "Respects their religion, too," Ben had said. "I think he'll do."

After that, things settled down, and Time moved in an even flow—until the day C Troop's transfer orders came through. They were going to Fort Laramie, Ben Westcott announced jubilantly, a fine high-living post for a captain and his bride. Easy duty, hunting and fishing, hops, balls, quadrilles, concerts, and parlor theatricals. Assignment to Laramie, he assured her, was a cavalryman's dream come true.

Julie had her misgivings about Fort Laramie, but she kept them to herself. Fort Wicked was home, the only home she had ever known. She resented Time taking her away from Fort Wicked, no matter what Laramie had to offer.

From the day Ben Westcott told her they were going to Fort Laramie, Time had scampered like a jackrabbit, and now, this morning, all of a sudden, had come to a dreadful stop.

C Troop was lining up down there by the creek, preparing for the march. She could hear the sergeants barking commands, and see that silly old yellow ambulance drawn up near the stables. Ben Westcott said it was for her. The march would last four or five days, he said, and she'd need it for sleeping quarters and for transport, if the weather turned bad. She'd laughed at him for that. She could ride a horse through rain or snow, and if he could roll up in a blanket and sleep under the sky, so could she.

Snow had fallen during the night, only a light sprinkling of it driven by high winds, but the sun was out again, the sky a glassy blue. Fragile banners of motionless clouds—like stopped Time—stretched from horizon to horizon, left there by passing blasts of wind, elongated in the after-calm.

She turned the pinto down around the barracks, looking back over her shoulder for a last glimpse of two parallel mounds in the fort's old burying ground. One mound was grassed over, the other was raw earth, both crystaled with a dusting of snow. She raised her hand in a gesture of farewell, fighting a flow of tears. Time had come to a stop forever for Maude and Brad.

As the pony picked its way along the familiar line of winter-deadened willows, she looked for the last time at the old trading post, its rear walls blackened and ugly from the fire, the sturdy trading room lonely and deserted, beaten by Time.

Time could be cruel, she thought, healing the heart with its passing, but cruel, too.

She saw Ben Westcott coming up to meet her, trotting his horse over a thin drifting of snow. He was wearing his slouchy old field hat, his red hair spraying out carelessly over his forehead, and she wondered why it was that when he smiled at her all the misery went out of her heart and Time began moving again.

"You've said your goodbyes?" His voice was gentle. He turned his horse, riding close beside the pinto, touching her hand lightly with his gauntlet.

"Yes." Her voice choked in her throat, and she turned her face away from him, ashamed to show her emotion.

"C Troop is ready to move out," he said. "You want to ride in the ambulance?"

"I'll ride with you."

He nodded, and led the way across the creek.

Five minutes later, the troop was moving. As soon as the column turned into the main trail and faced east, Westcott and Julie took a hundred-yard lead across the flats. On the high ridge off to the left were the tall pines she'd looked at every morning, marching down like soldiers. Now their green ranks were dusted with glistening snow.

She never looked back, keeping her face turned toward the winter sun. Time was moving in a dream. Ben Westcott was riding beside her, and she knew now for certain that where he was, was where she wanted to be.

About the Author

DEE BROWN is the author of several Western novels and a number of nonfiction books on various aspects of nineteenth-century Americana. His works include *Grierson's Raid, Creek Mary's Blood, Hear the Lonesome Whistle Blow,* and *Bury My Heart at Wounded Knee.* Born in Louisiana, Dee Brown entered the world of literature as a printer.

He now lives with his wife Sally in Little Rock, Arkansas.

THE OLD-TIMERS

These two grizzled knights of the Old West never listen when folks say they're over the hill—they just use their true grit, their know-how, and a little luck to tame even the meanest young outlaws.

- ☐ **THE OLD-TIMERS OF GUN SHY**
  16565-2 $2.95

- ☐ **THE OLD-TIMERS IN THE SANGRE DE CRISTOS**
  20032-6 $2.95

Return to the savage storm of VIETNAM in some of today's best novels.

__**CENTRIFUGE**
J.C. Pollock 11156-0 $3.95

__**CROSSFIRE**
J.C. Pollock 11602-3 $3.95

__**GOING AFTER CACCIATO**
Tim O'Brien 32965-3 $4.95

__**MISSION M.I.A.**
J.C. Pollock 15819-2 $3.95